5/07

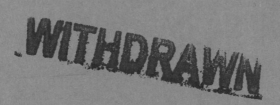

THE PASSAGE

A Freestone Publication

Published by
PEACHTREE PUBLISHERS
1700 Chattahoochee Avenue
Atlanta, Georgia 30318-2112

www.peachtree-online.com

Cover design by Loraine M. Joyner
Book design by Melanie McMahon Ives

Jacket photograph © iStockphoto/Gina Goforth
Jacket background image courtesy of Naval Historical Center

Manufactured in United States of America

10 9 8 7 6 5 4 3 2 1
First Edition

R. G. Skerrett painting of the CSS *Arkansas* on p. iii, J. Wells map of First Vicksburg Campaign on p. vi, and illustrations on pp. 248–49 courtesy of Naval Historical Center, Washington, D.C.

Library of Congress Cataloging-in-Publication Data

Killgore, James, 1959-
  The passage / by James Killgore. -- 1st ed.
    p. cm.
  Includes bibliographical references (p. 248)
  Summary: Fifteen-year-old Mississippi schoolboy Sam Wood learns about honor, courage, and friendship while serving on a Confederate ironclad gunboat, the CSS *Arkansas*, in the early days of the Civil War.
  ISBN 1-56145-384-6
  [1. *Arkansas* (Confederate ram)--Fiction. 2. United States--History--Civil War, 1861-1865--Fiction.] I. Title.
  PZ7.K5563Pas 2006
  [Fic]--dc22
                                                    2006012005

THE PASSAGE

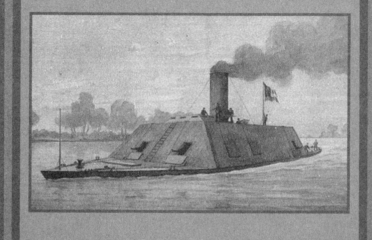

JAMES KILLGORE

Ω
PEACHTREE
ATLANTA

For Thomas Maxwell and
Aileen Marie (Lana) Killgore—my parents

I am grateful to the staff at Peachtree for their encouragement in the long gestation of this book. In particular I would like to thank Lisa Mathews, who guided the development of THE PASSAGE from proposal to outline to finished book. Her skill and experience in YA fiction have been invaluable. I would also like to thank Vicky Holifield for her expert and thoughtful editing of the manuscript.

My family also deserves major thanks for their support and patience— my children Emily and Max and my wife Ann, who helped in countless ways, including a close read of the first draft.

—J. K.

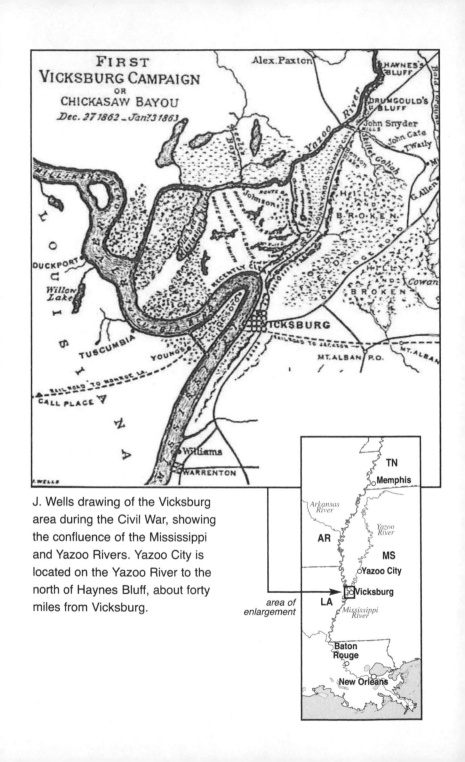

J. Wells drawing of the Vicksburg area during the Civil War, showing the confluence of the Mississippi and Yazoo Rivers. Yazoo City is located on the Yazoo River to the north of Haynes Bluff, about forty miles from Vicksburg.

1

My first glimpse of the CSS *Arkansas* was early one morning on the Yazoo River in the spring of 1862. The sun had not yet risen over the treetops and a thin mist lay on the water.

Cope Morgan and I were out checking trout lines near the mouth of Short Creek. We'd had a good catch: mainly catfish and white crappie, along with a couple of blue gill. Cope, who's a free Negro sharecropper on my grandfather's farm, knows all the best spots on the river. I was just pulling a big catfish into the skiff when I heard him exclaim:

"What in blazes...?"

I turned to find that a big side-wheel river steamer had appeared round the bend, plowing against the swift spring current. In tow behind it was a vessel the likes of which I'd never before seen. She was big, about a hundred ninety feet in length, sliding low through the river, gunwales just above the waterline like a barge. But unlike a barge, her bow was pointed as in a seagoing ship. A large wooden box sat mid-deck like an ark, with a sloping front and back and an iron smokestack poking out the top. She in turn towed a barge upon which lay stacks of rail iron and other large items covered in canvas tarp.

"What kinda boat is that?" asked Cope.

"Beats me," I replied.

But I swear, a curious chill ran through my bones at the sight. I knew somehow my fate would be bound up with that odd-looking vessel.

~

That afternoon Grandfather and I went into Yazoo City for the week's provisions.

The boat was the talk of the town. Word had spread from Frank Morris who works down at Liverpool Landing where the steamer had stopped to take on coal. The captain would say nothing, thinking old Frank a possible Yankee spy. But one of the crew had been made more agreeable with a bottle of bourbon. The CSS *Arkansas* was an unfinished ironclad, an armored gunboat like the Confederate *Virginia* that had fought the Yankee *Monitor* at Hampton Roads. When it looked certain Memphis would fall into Union hands, they had towed her from the shipyard down the Mississippi and up the Yazoo.

"They're taking it up to Greenwood," said Mr. Pendleton, owner of the mercantile. Reed Pendleton was one of the few people in Yazoo City still civil to

Grandfather since he left the church. "Much good it'll do us up there," he added.

"But how's she armed?" I asked. "And what about her captain and crew?"

Mr. Pendleton shrugged. "That's all I heard, Sam."

Just then Louisa Thurman came into the shop with her daughter Nancy. Tall and stiff in her customary gray, she walked straight to the far end of the counter and stood there imperiously, tapping a fingernail, without so much as a glance in our direction.

Mr. Pendleton sighed. "Excuse me, Reverend, Sam." He tightened his apron and shifted down the counter. "Afternoon, Louisa."

"Reed." She held out her list. "Just a few things."

Mr. Pendleton took the slip of paper and pushed down his bifocals. "Fine. Think we have all this, apart from the vanilla."

Mrs. Thurman snorted her disapproval but nodded. "Tell me, have you heard much of Justin?"

Mr. Pendleton flinched. His eldest son Justin had attended the University of Mississippi in Oxford up until the war broke out. He then joined the University Grays and was now marching somewhere in Virginia. Mr. Pendleton lived in constant anticipation of the postman, desperate for news but dreading the wrong kind.

"Just the occasional letter. Fine so far. Thank you."

"You must be so proud," said Mrs. Thurman loudly. "I only wish I had sons myself to offer the cause."

"Yes...well...," Mr. Pendleton stammered, waving the list. "I'll see to this now."

An awkward silence fell over the shop. I prayed Grandfather wouldn't say anything, but knew for certain he would. Just when Mr. Pendleton was out of earshot he spoke up.

"Fine sentiment, Louisa. But I can think of a no more welcome time not to have sons."

"Is that so, Reverend?" she replied without looking at him, fingering a piece of lace on the counter.

"Yes, unless one desires only anxiety and heartache."

"Well. I wouldn't expect *you* to understand that kind of sacrifice," Mrs. Thurman sniffed.

"Sacrifice, indeed," Grandfather said. "Should the reports be true, some 2,000 sons—nearly twice that, if you count Yankees—were sacrificed in a single day last month up at Shiloh."

Mrs. Thurman looked away again. "I read the newspapers."

"No doubt. My only point being that, as regards Reed, a son in theory is not quite the same as one of flesh and bone."

Just then her daughter risked a glance in my direction. Was she as mortified as I? Nancy was the second youngest of the Thurman girls and the prettiest. She and I had once swum together practically nude in Piney Creek and then shared a sweet kiss, or so I'm told, the occasion being my third birthday. In any case, I was spared further discomfort when Tom Pendleton,

Justin's younger brother, arrived back at the counter with our order. Grandfather settled the bill.

"You have a fine afternoon, ladies," he said as we left. Mrs. Thurman turned away without reply.

It was her husband Douglas Thurman who'd apparently drafted the letter to Bishop Hall asking that Grandfather be replaced as rector at Christ Episcopal. All eight elders signed it, and Bishop Hall made Grandfather travel by train all the way to Birmingham just to discuss the issue. In the letter they accused him of using the gospel as a pretext for his known abolitionist and anti-secessionist views.

Or, as Grandfather put it: "Preaching such radical notions as 'blessed are the meek' and 'all men are equal in the eyes of God'."

In the end he resigned, less in protest than disgust. At least he could spend more time tending his peach orchard. But attitudes in town were hard against him. I feared one day he'd say too much and attract worse trouble.

On the journey back to Sandhill, I was so angry I refused to speak. How could Grandfather not see what people thought of us now? How could he not understand that so many of them hated us? It was a hot, clear evening and our mare Sloeberry toiled up the hill out of town.

Grandfather sighed. "Sure is quiet, Sloe."

The horse pricked her ears.

"Makes the road seem long, don't it?"

I said nothing.

Grandfather sighed again: "Guess you're angry at me for embarrassing you in front of Nancy Thurman. She is a pretty girl."

I couldn't hold my anger in any longer. "Why can't you just keep quiet? You know they're calling you a traitor in town, don't you?"

Grandfather nodded. "And what do you think?"

"We are at war," I told him, "even if you don't approve."

"I suppose you also think I'm wrong for not letting a fifteen-year-old boy run off to Jackson and join up?"

This had been a dispute between us ever since the first shot fired at Fort Sumter. All around the South, armies were on the march, the world was turned upside down, and here I was riding home in the same old tired wagon as countless Saturdays before. I found myself shaking with frustration.

"I'm not a boy," I informed him. "I'll be sixteen next month. Almost everyone I know has joined or is planning to. Why not me?"

"Indeed, why you?"

A typical response from Grandfather, even the simplest conversation a Socratic dialogue.

"Because it's the only honorable thing to do," I said.

"So is that what all this killing's about—honor?"

"No! It's not just that," I said. "We have to stand up for our rights."

"That so?" Grandfather replied, tugging at his beard. "And which particular right, being so deprived of, do you think is worth trading your life for?"

I couldn't come up with a good reply. Mr. Fitzhugh, our schoolmaster, said it all so much better.

Grandfather laid a hand on my knee. "Might be worth considering, that question."

Near Barlow Farms, as if to add to my frustration, we saw a cloud of dust rising on the road ahead. A cavalry unit rode toward us on its way to Yazoo City. None of your ragtag local bushwhackers, this was a regular Confederate army unit, probably detached from Van Dorn's force at Vicksburg. Grandfather pulled the wagon off the road to give way. A red-bearded captain dressed in gray with yellow trim and a plumed slouch hat led the column. He nodded to Grandfather as he passed.

On came the rest of the unit at a fast trot, hooves making a soft thunder on the dusty ground, gear rattling in their saddlebags. Most of the riders took no notice of us, but down the line I met the gaze of a young face, a soldier not much older than me, judging by his scant mustache. He rode a tall chestnut horse and looked all the part in brown, knee-length cavalry boots, a gray coat with polished brass buttons, with saber and scabbard swinging loose from his belt. Passing, he smiled at me and touched the brim of his hat—such an elegant, superior gesture that it left me undecided as to whether I wanted to pull him off his horse and beat him senseless or trade places with him right then, body and soul.

As the final rider went by, Grandfather pulled the wagon back onto the road. The raised dust of their passage stung our eyes.

On reaching home I jumped from the wagon and went straight inside, leaving Grandfather to unhitch Sloeberry, a thing I'd never done before. I found Martha and Liz in the parlor, and slumped into a chair in a foul silence. Martha, my older sister, held a letter just arrived that day from her fiancé Henry. My younger sister Liz was, as always, making herself intensely annoying, clumping about the room in her block shoe (on account of being born with one leg too short). She wore an old silk waistcoat of our father's and brandished a bamboo cane like a sword. Her long, dark hair was tied tightly in a bun and her pale cheeks flushed with effort.

"A hit, a palpable hit!" she cried.

"Who are you supposed to be?" I asked.

"Hamlet," she answered and swung the cane toward me. "Come, Laertes: you but dally. Pass with your best violence." She assumed a fencing stance and waved the tip a few inches from my face.

I tried to ignore this. "Wouldn't Ophelia or Juliet be more appropriate for a girl?"

She lurched away and began to parry with one of Grandmother's rosewood chairs. "How dull," she groaned. "Miss Tompkins says that in Shakespeare's time all the female parts were acted by boys. So I don't see why in modern times a girl can't play Hamlet."

With that she feigned being stabbed and raised a hand to her brow. "O villainy. I am dead. Adieu. Sweet Horatio. Adieu."

She collapsed to the floor.

From her chair Martha snapped, "Could you do that elsewhere? It's very distracting."

Liz stayed dead a moment longer before sitting up and sighing. "It's just another letter from Henry. O *Hen*-ry, of what doth thy name speaketh? Warm hugs, loving kisses, fresh eggs..."

She burst into laughter. No one finds Liz more witty than Liz. Getting no response from Martha or me, she struggled up from the floor. "Grumpy old bores." And she limped off to bother Bessie in the kitchen.

Martha paid no notice, turning over the last page of the letter.

"Anything interesting to report?" I asked.

She seemed not to hear at first, but finally looked up. "Sorry?" A tear ran down her cheek.

"What's wrong?" I asked.

She dabbed her eyes with a sleeve. "Here. Read for yourself."

I was only ever given selected pages of Henry's letters. He seemed to know this and would sometimes address comments to me: "...the 13-inch mortar lobs a 200-pound shell (Sam)..." or "Sam might be interested to know the ship's draft—19 feet." But I suspect he also sought to impress Martha with his military talk.

Henry wrote then from Mobile. He was a corporal with the Confederate Corps of Engineers, building earthworks to guard the harbor. He'd enlisted just after the war broke out, coming home from his second year studying mathematics at Princeton. Two days before reporting for duty, he presented himself on our front porch in his best suit and asked for a private word with Grandfather. Martha could have had the choice of any number of suitors in Yazoo County, yet she favored bookish Henry Brooks, with his round, bottle-bottom spectacles, thinning hair, and wide backside.

Liz was appalled. "Not Henry! Have you a fever? Are you delirious?"

Martha replied, simply, "No. I love him."

And that was that. They would wed as soon as the war was over. It was a good match. Martha would never be happy married to some lazy planter's son with little conversation beyond horse racing and hunting dogs. And she'd known Henry all her life, the Brooks being neighbors back when we lived in town.

Henry wrote twice a week without fail, always four pages. No matter that nothing much seemed to happen there outside of the occasional Yankee gunboat steaming into range to lob a few shells. Each letter was composed under the delusion (or so it seemed to me then) that love demands great fascination in tedious details: how many slices of bacon eaten at breakfast; the day's weather; every blister, cut, and runny nose suffered; a cloud "shaped in the profile of George Washington—all remarked on the likeness." And yet Martha devoured every word.

But this letter was different. Henry had written to say that Billy McDermott was dead. He was a cousin of Henry's from Jackson who used to spend a few weeks each summer in Yazoo City. I must admit that I could barely stand the boy. He liked to pretend Jackson was some booming metropolis and we were all just country bumpkins.

Liz took great delight in imitating his tired drawl: "Well, over in Jackson we never suck jelly through our teeth—it just isn't done. Neither do we belch nor break wind."

Martha would scold her for being rude. She thought Billy quite dashing.

Henry wrote that Billy had been wounded at Shiloh and left behind in Corinth when Beauregard's forces retreated South. No one expected him to die. Judge McDermott himself rode the two hundred miles to the town and secured a pass from the Yankee commander to search for his son. Wounded and dying men languished everywhere: the railway station, hotels, schools, churches. But Billy had already succumbed to pneumonia a week previous and had been buried in a mass grave.

It was shocking news. I felt angry. Maybe not as angry as I might if he'd been a good friend. But now it was a personal matter, this war. I vowed to myself then and there to avenge the death of Billy McDermott. Even if he was a prig, I figured he was worth at least a dozen Yankees.

No one was much in the mood for conversation as we sat down to dinner that night. Bessie had batter-fried the catfish Cope and I caught that morning. Grandfather motioned for the blessing and we joined hands.

"Dear Lord. Thank you for the food on our table and the countless blessings you bestow upon us," he began, as always. "We are your children and but dust without your love...."

But then he paused, as if at a loss for words. Just a few seconds, yet it seemed much longer.

"Lord. These are sad, desperate times, but of course you see all. To think of a young man like Billy, the loss to his family, it's almost too much to bear..."

Martha squeezed my hand tight.

"Help us to understand, Lord, to see we have a choice. None of this is preordained. We pray that your grace ease the sad burden of pain, sorrow, fear and grief on all those suffering—families and soldiers—on both sides of the divide. For you are God to all: a paradox without answer, unless by faith. We ask in thy name. Amen."

And they all said "Amen" but I just couldn't. He'd meant it for me, that prayer, or so I thought. Yet I felt nothing but outrage. To ask God to ease the burden of Billy's family in the same breath as that of his killers? And to talk about *choice?* The Yankees had a choice: not to invade our land, not to trample upon our most cherished values, and so on. I forget all the arguments now.

~

Three weeks later, just a few days before the start of summer holidays, I arrived at school one Monday morning to find the place in a state of high excitement. Albert met me at the gate.

"You heard the news? That turtle boat is back down from Greenwood, moored at the boatyard. They're gonna case her out in iron. She's gonna sink every Yankee ship in the Mississippi!"

Albert Ledbetter was my best and oldest friend. That spring he was also my only friend. It doesn't take much to become a marked man at school. All that bad business with Grandfather and the church had made me an outcast at Yazoo Academy. My chief tormentor was Wade Walton. I never before paid much mind to him or his gang: Jack Butler, Frank Davis, and a few other scrawny hangers-on. Nor they to me. Mostly they picked on other poor souls like Paul Jacobson, whose daddy was a Jew, or Franklin Carter, a pale, delicate boy who was the prettiest in a family with three sisters. It must have been a great relief to them when Walton turned his malice on me.

Walton held court on the thick worn roots of a giant live oak in the front school yard. That morning he and his boys sat there as usual, waiting for the bell. The whistling started just as I entered the gate: "Yankee Doodle Dandy" performed in time to my walking pace. When I slowed or stopped, so did the whistling, only to start up again as I hurried into the main building. I might have found it funny if the joke hadn't been on me.

Inside the classroom Mr. Fitzhugh struggled to establish order. He banged loudly on the podium with his "equalizer," the name he used for his cane rod. Mr. Fitzhugh was a small man, smaller than a good number of his students.

"All right now. Gentlemen! Cicero. *De Republica.* Get out your texts. Page 231. Who would like to read the second paragraph?"

In past days I would have raised my hand and likely been chosen. I was the best Latin scholar in the school, if I say so myself. Fitzhugh also used to give me extra tutelage in Greek. He first raised the possibility of my one day going up North to study at Dartmouth College, just as he had done from a small town in North Louisiana. But even Fitzhugh's attitude had changed. He avoided my gaze and no longer called on me in class.

Duncan Wilson raised his hand. He was a country boy from Tula Springs and not well known for his intellectual curiosity. Fitzhugh looked dubious. "Wilson? Are you actually volunteering?"

The boy grinned. "Oh. No sir. I mean we were all just wondering. What do you reckon of that boat, sir?"

Fitzhugh raised an eyebrow. "Did you all catch that? Our yeoman farmer here would like to know what I *reckon.*"

The class laughed. Wilson's big ears turned bright red and he grinned even broader.

Walton raised his hand. "What I think he means, sir, is how do you rate the gunboat's chances now that New Orleans has surrendered and the Union fleet is heading up the Mississippi?"

"Well, thank you for clarifying that point, Mr. Walton. And I'm terribly sorry to disappoint you gentlemen in your efforts to divert my attention from the writings of Cicero. But the Town Council, of which I am secretary, has been sworn to secrecy in regard to this topic. Vital information could get into the wrong hands. I will say this much, though: She's ably commanded by a highly experienced officer from Grenada, whom I've already met. A veteran of the Mexican War and a consummate professional, hopefully as inventive as his namesake: Captain Isaac Newton Brown."

~

Albert and I headed over to the boatyard just after school. Armed sentries had been posted at the entrance gate and no one was allowed to pass. Albert ran home to get his father's field glasses, and we climbed a tall elm on the edge of a field across the road. A foolish act in retrospect, as we might have been shot for spies.

A large encampment had been set up in the boatyard. A half dozen smoking blacksmith forges rang with the sound of beaten iron. A team of oxen arrived with another forge as we watched. At the center of activity was the boat itself, moored to the bank, men working on her box-like casemate, shirts stripped off in the heat. A second boat, the river steamer *Capitol*, lay alongside her and rattled with the sound of drills boring holes into the rail iron for the bolts used to fasten it to the wooden hull as armor.

As we watched, a team of workmen struggled with

ropes to maneuver a heavy engine component, suspended from the *Capitol*'s bale crane, down into an open hatchway of the gunboat. A man in a blue uniform, with dark hair and a dark beard, appeared on the bow of the steamer to watch this operation. He stood alone, unmistakably in command.

I handed the field glasses back to Albert, who asked, "Is that him?"

I nodded. "Looks the part."

"Think his parents had high expectations?"

"No doubt," I replied. I didn't mention to Albert then how the name Isaac Newton Brown was already familiar to me. My father had sometimes mentioned Brown when speaking of the men he served with in the Mexican War. My father was not a topic I liked to bring up. Not even to Albert.

It was then that the idea first occurred to me—as I sat watching with envy all those soldiers and sailors, those men of purpose. It was an idea that would soon grant me my wish—a bellyful of war—and drag poor Albert along for the passage.

2

Next morning I was late for school, thanks to Liz fussing over some fool ribbon for her hair. Cope let me off at the crossroads and whipped away with the buggy to get Liz off to the girl's academy by eight-thirty. I dashed the remaining quarter mile to school and arrived just as Jakes rang the bell for first period. Fitzhugh was still in his cupboard. I should have noticed something was up; the room was too quiet. I flipped open my desktop to get out my jotter. Inside lay a crumpled pair of ladies' cotton underbreeches. The class erupted in laughter. There was no doubting who was behind it.

I shoved my desk away and marched to the back of the room where Walton sat, and thrust the drawers under his nose. The fury I felt was almost a relief. "So I suppose you think this a fine joke," I said.

Walton shrugged. "Looks more like a pair of bloomers to me."

More laughter. I felt the blood rising into my face. "How did they get in my desk?"

"How should I know, Wood? None of my business what you keep in there. Dog-eared copy of *Uncle Tom's Cabin*? Your black mammy's old head rag?"

Walton's sidekick, Jack Butler, then piped up: "Try 'em on, Wood. Maybe they'll fit."

I ignored him. Butler hadn't the wit to come up with such a prank. Besides that, he was built like a double-walled brick outhouse. I threw the bloomers into Walton's face. "So are you saying I'm a coward? On top of all the other lies you're telling behind my back?"

Walton snorted. "What lies? You mean you don't love the niggers?"

I was climbing over his desk before I even realized it. Walton fell backward in his chair and began to scramble away across the floor. Someone grabbed me hard by the shoulder. Without thinking I swung a wild punch and caught the offender solid on the cheek. Of course it had to be big Jack Butler. He grabbed the knot of my tie and twisted it tight, a look of disbelief on his face.

"You hit me," he growled.

A roar of excitement arose from the class at the prospect of my immediate murder. Fitzhugh rushed from his cupboard at the sound and pushed through the knot of boys.

"Butler! Let go of Wood. What's going on here?"

Troy Davis chimed in: "Wood punched him, sir. Right in the face."

"Thank you, Mr. Davis. Not that I asked for witnesses. Is that true, Wood?"

"Yes sir."

There was no point trying to explain about the bloomers. It wouldn't make any difference.

Fitzhugh raised an eyebrow. "The 'why' is implied, Mr. Wood."

"We had a disagreement."

He smiled as he considered this. "Have you anything to add, Butler?"

"No, sir."

Fitzhugh puffed himself up. He looked grave, though you could tell he was enjoying himself. "Well, as you both know, I do not allow brawling in my classroom. It is ungentlemanly and antithetical to the ethos of this academy."

I had heard this speech before and knew where it was heading.

"But what happens," he continued, "out of the bounds and off the grounds of this institution is not strictly my concern. I am now returning to my study. Jakes will ring the bell again in another fifteen minutes, at which time I expect this matter to be resolved so that we can carry on afresh with the day's work."

Fitzhugh turned and walked out of the classroom.

A shout went up: "Bull pit! Bull pit! Bull pit!"

Three or so boys grabbed me and I was carried along in the rush of the mob. Butler grinned at me as he, too, was pulled out the door. Out in the corridor junior boys crowded into the doorways of the other classrooms to see what all the noise was about. I caught sight of Mr. Anders, the science and mathematics master, pushing his way into the hall. He watched in disgust as the shouting mob passed.

The bull pit was a flattened hollow in the woods out back of the Academy. There Yazoo boys gathered at the noontime recess to smoke and cuss and spit and do generally anything else not allowed on campus. There by ritual they also came to fight.

The gleeful mob pushed us out the doors of the main building. I shook off the hands holding me and made my own way to the back gate. Albert caught up beside me.

"Will I second you?" he asked.

"Thanks," I replied, as I undid my tie and took off my coat. Albert folded them both over his arm.

"A little advice," Albert whispered. "Butler'll murder you. Just take a few hits and fall over."

"I appreciate your confidence."

Albert frowned. "What else you gonna do?"

"I don't know," I said honestly.

~

A ring of boys three-deep had formed around the patch of bare clay soil. Walton seconded Butler. He only smirked in my direction, relieved, I think, that it was Butler's fight and not his. Butler looked huge without his coat and collar, his neck and shoulders broad like an Angus bull's.

"Let's get at it, Wood," he said, and stepped out into the ring.

Until then I hadn't thought much about strategy. My only possible advantage was in being smarter. I figured surprise offered the best hope. A bold opening might just catch him off guard. So when Butler turned to make some comment to Walton I ducked my head and ran straight at his gut.

But Butler proved as agile as he was big. At the last moment he danced aside and spun about on one foot, and with the other delivered a hard kick to my backside. I landed face-first in the dirt. Peals of laughter erupted from the mob.

Butler's move was a mistake, though, if he reckoned on coming out untouched. I saw red. While he was enjoying his joke I stood up, planted both feet, and landed a fist square in his face. It hurt, too. Butler backed away with his eyes closed, head bowed. His hand came away from his nose covered in blood.

That was the last blow I landed in that fight. Butler recovered quickly and with a few punches had me pinned to the ground. There he pounded my face until Jakes sounded the bell and three guys had to pull him off me, or so Albert later reported.

Albert helped me back to the school building. As I came through the main doors I looked up and saw Fitzhugh watching from the window of his study. His expression was blank, empty. But I no longer cared.

Just inside the corridor we met Anders waiting in the doorway of his physics lab. He sent Albert back to class and took me by the arm up the stairs to his study. He sat me in a chair by the window to better inspect my face.

"You're a mess, son," he said. "How did this start?"

"Somebody put a pair of bloomers in my desk."

Anders sighed. "So shall we reap what we sow."

I wasn't sure I'd heard right. "Sir?"

"Never mind," he said. "Let's get you cleaned up."

Anders had taught mathematics and natural sciences at the Academy since its founding. Tall and white-haired, with long thin arms and legs, he was known variously among the boys as "Pretzel," "Bug Legs," or "Uncle Sam," mostly out of affection. He was well liked and enthusiastic about everything he taught. No student was ever discounted, no matter how hopeless.

Five years ago when old Mr. Trent retired, everyone had assumed that Anders would take over as headmaster. But the job had instead gone to Fitzhugh, much the younger of the two. Maybe it was because Anders was a Yankee, having moved from Delaware to Yazoo City more than twenty years earlier. But Grandfather said it was because he had no time for petty, small-town politics—unlike Fitzhugh, who curried favor with every rich landowner in Yazoo County. All I knew was that fights in Anders' class never ended in the bull pit.

Anders had to return to his first period physics class, but he let me stay on in his study to recover my wits. It was a small room with one wall shelved entirely with books and other objects: rocks and mineral samples, fossil shells, old Indian relics, animal skulls, a large hornet's nest, a stuffed armadillo in a glass case.

A mirror hung over the fireplace. I got up to have a look at my face. It was a mess. My lip was busted, nostrils crusted with blood. A black and purple bruise had formed over my left eye, which had nearly swollen shut. But to tell the truth, I hadn't felt better in months.

It seemed as if a divide had been crossed in my life. Looking at my battered face, it was as though I had already joined the war, been bloodied in battle. Anything now was justified. It made the plan then hatching in my brain seem less like some desperate fantasy, less like a boy dreaming he might steal away to join the circus.

I touched the bruise over my eye and winced. But the pain felt good. Not like the dull aching dread I felt every day before going to school. Gazing back into that mirror, I found myself grinning like an idiot.

Fitzhugh never looked in my direction at next period Latin. But it was no matter. Soon I hoped never to see him or Yazoo Academy again. I wrote a note and passed it to Albert.

Prichard's Cave after school.

He gave me a quizzical look but nodded.

~

Our town sits on a bend of the Yazoo River where the Mississippi hill country gives way to the broad flat delta. To the west across the river, far as the eye can see, lies swampy bottomland. To the east the land rises steeply into rolling uplands. Those hills skirt the twisted course of the Yazoo all the way to its conflu-ence with the Mississippi River above Vicksburg. There they form the high promontories and bluffs that then bristled with Confederate cannon in command of the great river, bombarding any Union boat that dared pass.

After school that day Albert and I headed up into the hills. It was hot, but a fresh breeze made it seem less so as we climbed the Bell Road. We didn't talk much while we walked. Albert knew I had something important to say, but he let me get to it in my own time. Just as we passed the last of the houses, he pulled out a paper bag of red licorice rope and tore off a strand for me. We chewed in silence. Near the brow of the hill we stopped for a breather and looked back across to the cotton fields that lined the far side of the river. A couple of wagons sat parked in the shade of an large oak tree. A few slaves moved among the fur-rows. Planting had just finished.

Fitzhugh liked to preach to us in class about how it was pure envy that started the war. Not just of the wealth we drew from those fields—cotton, sugarcane, rice—but envy of our culture, our civilization, our way of life. The North, he said, was a nation of dark factories, of shopkeepers and mechanics, of bloodless Puritans without honor or dignity. A Southern soldier was worth ten Yankees, he'd told us, and that was how we'd prevail in the war even though we were outnumbered. Fitzhugh was a blowhard, but lots of men in town talked that way in the early days of the war. Later, after Shiloh and some of the other battles, with thousands dead on both sides, I heard less such talk.

I didn't know what to believe. But one thing I did know for certain: every able-bodied young man in town over the age of eighteen was expected to join up and fight or be branded a coward. Most of the boys in my class would soon be old enough to enlist, within a year or two if the war lasted that long. But I didn't intend to wait.

Old Man Prichard had nailed a hand-painted Keep Out sign to a tree trunk at the head of the trail. "No huntin'. No kids," Albert read out loud.

Just then two bluetick hounds began to bay from the farmhouse a quarter mile up the road. They had to have smelled us. Albert ducked into the woods and I followed, both us of laughing like fools as we ran up the trail.

It twisted up the ridge among hickory and beech and oak, some trees centuries old with thick, knotted trunks and broad canopies. Years ago we used to go there almost every day to play—Robin Hood in Sherwood Forest, or Washington and his Continental Army doing battle with the Redcoats, or pirates of the Caribbean with a giant fallen oak as our galleon. But as Albert and I got older we went there less and less often. A year at least had passed since I'd last set foot on the ridge. It seemed a lonely place to me that afternoon, almost forlorn, haunted by the ghosts of our younger selves.

The trail to the cave followed the ridge a ways and then dropped down a steep-sided gully. Albert walked ahead, slipping and sliding over the loose dirt in his school brogans. He was near enough six feet tall then, slim as a beanpole, all arms and legs, forever knocking into things and tripping over his own feet. Two years earlier he'd been the runt of the class, but then almost overnight he'd gained two inches on me. This pleased him no end, for people had often assumed he was my baby brother. We'd been friends since before either of us could remember. Mrs. Ledbetter and my mother had grown up like sisters in neighboring houses. Albert was born only eight days before me. As babies we shared the same playpen, lulled by the sound of our mothers' gossip and laughter.

Sarah, the Ledbetters' old mammy, always said that as a toddler I talked non-stop while Albert barely said a word before age five.

"Child had no need, you always answering for him. 'Albert wants his potty' or 'Albert needs a nap' or 'No peas for Albert, he hates peas.'"

And that pretty much set the pattern growing up, me doing most of the talking. Even schoolteachers used to let me answer for Albert, him being so quiet and shy.

"Fifty-nine is the sum, ma'am. He's written it on his slate."

"Thank you, Sam. That's correct, Albert."

Albert's silence annoyed Mrs. Ledbetter no end, as she herself was a champion talker.

"Speak up, boy," she'd snap at her son. "Devil snatch your tongue?"

I think she worried that maybe Albert was slow or something. That is, until he started to win every class medal going for math and science. The prizes never stopped coming. Anders told Grandfather that Albert was the finest student he'd come across in thirty-five years of teaching. That he deserved to be at Harvard or Yale.

～

"They'll have us arrested when they find out," Albert said when I told him my plan.

"Maybe that, or make us walk the plank."

Albert held his candle at an angle. Melted wax dripped and beaded on the sandy floor of the chamber. Its flame sputtered and flickered on the low ceiling. Prichard's Cave was a short tunnel dug into the hard dirt of a dried-up stream gully. It opened at the end into a small, dark cell. No one knew who dug it out or why or how long ago. Maybe ancient Indians or a long-dead trapper. Carved into the walls were generations of Yazoo City graffiti, including my own father's initials:

SJW 1832

I fingered the markings. Had he, too, come here to dream of going off to sea, to war?

"I thought you wanted to join the cavalry," Albert said.

"I plan to, after we clear out the Union Navy."

"Unless of course they make you admiral."

"I might stay then."

Albert grinned. "What if you get killed?"

The words fell flat in the dead air. Albert looked immediately regretful. I stretched over and kicked his ankle. "What kind of stupid question is that? If I die, then I'll hover over your pillow on my gossamer wings and keep you awake with my damned harp."

"I'll swat you with my Bible."

We both laughed and I leaned forward into the light. "So are you with me?"

"Aren't I always?" Albert replied, and then looked up with a grimace. "Butler sure did a job on your face. Looks even worse by candlelight."

"You're too kind," I said.

~

Bessie had dinner on the table when I made it home. I closed the front door quietly and tried to sneak up the stairs. But at the first creak of a floorboard Grandfather called out from the dining room.

"Are you joining us, Sam?"

"Down in a minute."

I went up to my room and changed my blood-stained shirt and cleaned up best I could. Martha gasped when she saw my face.

"Sam! What happened?"

Liz sniggered. "More to the point, who won?"

"Hush, Liz," Grandfather snapped.

"You take your seat now, Sam. Food's getting cold."

No one spoke for the rest of the meal, though Liz kept stealing glances in my direction. Later that evening Grandfather came up to my room as I was doing my Latin homework. He stood in the doorway.

"Sam. Whatever happened, I'm sorry. It's not fair that you have to suffer for my choices. People can be ignorant that way."

"What makes you think this had anything to do with you?" I lied. "Not everything's about you."

I'd never spoken to Grandfather like that before. But he didn't check me or get angry.

"I just assumed—" he began.

"—that everyone thinks I'm a coward and a traitor to boot."

He shook his head and sighed. "Like I said—it's not fair and I am sorry. I'll let you get back to your studies."

I immediately regretted my words. Hurting Grandfather didn't make me feel any better; it only increased my frustration. I found it impossible to concentrate on schoolwork after that. My head felt tight, like an overwound clock. So I left my books and went out for a walk. The moon hung high and bright in the night sky like a cold, gray stone. I headed down the drive toward Cope's cabin and found him out on his porch having a smoke.

"Heard you been fighting," he said.

I dropped into the rocking chair beside him. "Yeah. Jack Butler."

Cope whistled under his breath. "That's one big boy."

"Don't I know it."

"What ya'll fighting about?"

I told him the full story but left out the bit about "loving the niggers." It bothered me that out of all the crap I took from Walton, such a stupid comment should tip me over the edge. I wouldn't know how to explain that to Cope. Both he and Bessie had been slaves up until seven years ago when old Mrs. Armstrong died and willed her entire household contents to the church: two human beings listed on an inventory, just like another set of chairs or a butter churn. Grandfather immediately had an attorney in town draw up papers to free them both. That's when the trouble really began. Some of the elders accused him of giving away church property. Grandfather asked how a church could own people, and that was that. Cope came to work for us, running the farm and tending the orchard. Grandfather hired Bessie to cook and keep house. I could never think of them as niggers or slaves.

Cope tapped his pipe clean on the edge of the porch and repacked it for another smoke. The tobacco had a sweet molasses smell. "Sure hope this war ends quick one way or another," he said. "Folks thinking crazy, acting crazy. You need to watch your back, Sam, and the reverend's, too."

"Why should I?" I shrugged. "It's his own fault."

Cope sat up in his rocker. "Shame on you. I won't

hear none of that. Your grandfather's the finest man in all Mississippi."

"Yeah, yeah." I'd heard it all before, and not just from Cope.

"I mean it, too," he added. "No matter what they say in town." Cope shook his head and said nothing for a few minutes. I got up to leave. He leaned back in the rocker again and stretched out his legs. "How about we tie out the gill net this Friday evening, catch us some more catfish?"

I stepped off the porch back into the darkness. There was no point involving him in my schemes. He might even tell Grandfather.

"Sorry," I replied. "Got other plans."

3

Two soldiers stood guard at the entrance to the boatyard that next afternoon. Albert and I hung back in the trees across the road to pluck up our courage. I decided to approach the guard on the right, a big man with a short, neat beard and a definite air of authority. The other guard appeared not much older than us, his uniform baggy and ill-fitting, forage cap pushed back off his forehead revealing a shock of lank, straw-colored hair.

In my hand I held the note that Albert and I had long agonized over earlier that day at school, not that anyone reading it would ever guess. The envelope was addressed to Captain Brown and the message read:

Sir,
Greetings. I trust you remember the name. I desire urgently to speak with you in regard to your current endeavor. I await at the gate.
      Yours,
      Sam Wood

Albert was sure we'd end up in the brig. It did seem, even to me, pretty lame as plans go. But there was no turning back. Both guards watched as we approached, the young one with an air of boredom, the other with stiff severity. I held out the envelope to him and said, "An important message for Captain Brown, sir."

He made no move to take it from me, just stared down at my outstretched hand in what seemed like contempt. The younger guard spoke up: "What kind of message?"

I turned to face him. "Well...it's a p-personal matter," I stuttered.

"Is it now? And what sort of personal message would Captain Brown be interested in coming from you?"

"I can't say. It's also highly confidential."

The soldier grinned. "Oh, from Jeff Davis himself?"

I tried not to lose my nerve. "No sir. But you can be assured the captain will be most displeased to learn I was turned away without passing this on as instructed."

"Most displeased," he mimicked. "Why, you damn puppy."

But I could I see that he was mulling over the possible consequences.

"Wallace," he barked at the big guard. "Keep an eye on these two while I take this over to the clerk."

He snatched the envelope from my hand and headed into the compound. The three of us stood waiting in silence. Albert pulled out his licorice and offered the open bag to the big guard. Almost instantly the stiff formality vanished. Wallace grinned broadly, revealing two missing front teeth.

"Thank you. I like licorice." He spoke with slow deliberateness. Tearing off a big piece, he began to chew happily. Albert took an interest in his old flint-lock musket.

Wallace held it out. "Want a look?"

Albert raised an eyebrow at me. "Sure. Thanks." He lifted the gun and aimed it up at the sky. He was just taking a bead on a passing crow when the younger guard returned.

"Wallace! What in hell are you doing?"

"Eating licorice. Want some, Hector?"

"Take back your damned gun. If Sarge sees that he'll have you strapped to the wheel. You're just about thick as a stump."

Albert handed back the musket. Wallace shoul-dered it quickly and stood stiffly at attention again, nearly choking on a wad of licorice.

Hector turned back to us. "That's your note deliv-ered to the clerk. Now beat it."

Albert turned to leave, but I hesitated. "Mind if we wait over by the road? We expect an answer."

Hector snorted. "Fine with me. But don't hold your breath."

Not five minutes later an officer in a blue naval uni-form appeared at the gate. Hector snapped to atten-tion and then pointed over to us. "You two!" the officer called out. "Follow me."

THE PASSAGE

We ran back across the road. Albert tripped jumping over the small ditch and I stopped to give him a hand up. The officer looked on with sour impatience. No more than nineteen or twenty, I figured. He stood a good head shorter than Albert, with thin, dark hair and a pale, hollow face covered in pimples. Over his upper lip he sported a scant growth of whiskers that looked more milk than moustache. He turned and strode away even before we reached the gate.

I gave Hector a wink as we passed, though he pretended not to see it.

The pale officer moved at too fast a pace for us to take in all the activity in the compound. A row of blacksmith forges roared and belched steam against the din of the smiths pounding out iron plating. A brigade of carpenters worked with chisels and saws, fashioning oak and pine fittings for the boat. Machinists stood at temporary lathes, tooling parts for the engines. Albert and I then got our first close glimpse of the *Arkansas* herself. We craned our necks as we passed, trying to take in every detail. Shirtless men hung by ropes down the wooden sides of the casemate, bolting on the rail iron armor. Another crew worked at the guide ropes securing her towering smokestack. All the while the pale officer said not a single word to us.

A sailor holding a musket jumped to attention as we reached the gangplank of the river steamer *Capitol*, which served as base for the crew working on the *Arkansas*. The officer led the way onto the boat and up an oak-paneled staircase to the staterooms on the boiler deck. Opening a door to one of the rooms, he called, "Sir. Your visitors."

From within a voice replied, "Thank you, Mr. Scales."

The officer held open the door for us, and Captain Brown rose from his desk as we entered. Up close the man was shorter than I expected. He wore a well-tailored "Old Navy" blue uniform, as did all the officers, and had neatly trimmed black hair and a beard. His face was lean, almost gaunt, with a long, thin nose. But what I noticed most were his eyes: clear blue, with a cold directness that seemed to measure you up in a single glance.

He looked beyond Albert, rightly expecting someone else. But when the door shut and he realized it was only us, he turned those cold eyes on me.

"So who are you?"

My throat went dry and I lost my voice.

"Speak up, boy!"

"Sam Wood. Sir," I managed to croak.

The eyes flashed. "Don't play games with me. You're not Samuel Wood."

"Junior, sir. You served with my father in Mexico?"

He pondered this a moment. I felt my face burning red.

"Where is your father now?"

"He's dead. Sir."

If he felt any sympathy it wasn't apparent. "How?"

"Six years ago, in an accident on the Mississippi. He was on a steamer headed for New Orleans. A child fell overboard. He jumped in to save her. They were both swept under."

I couldn't tell if he believed the lie. It sounded even more absurd spoken out loud, like a scene from some penny dreadful. Maybe he already knew the truth. But then why agree to see us?

The captain shook his head slowly and said, "I'm sorry to hear that."

Then the eyes again.

"So why are you here, Mr. Sam Wood Junior? Now that you've bluffed your way into my office." He folded his arms and leaned back on his desk.

This was my only chance. I knew I had to make it good.

"To enlist, sir. To serve on the *Arkansas*. You see, it was my father's firm wish that I pursue a career in the navy. That I go to Annapolis and train to be an officer. But then he died and now with the war it just seems impossible. So when I saw the *Arkansas* I thought there might be a chance to make good by my daddy."

Brown considered this a moment but looked no more convinced. "I did know your father," he said finally. "A good man. But *you* I don't know from horse crap. And what I've seen so far ain't too impressive."

He returned to his desk and picked up a pen. He dipped it into a cut-glass inkwell and began to scrawl a note as he spoke. "But it does so happen we're in need of a couple more boys. How old are you?"

"Seventeen," I replied.

He looked up with tired impatience.

"Nearly," I added.

"You're under age. So you'll need to come back here tomorrow with a letter from a legal guardian granting permission to enlist. That would be your mother, I suppose. Was it Clara?"

"Yes sir. But my mother passed away a year before my father's accident. My grandfather looks after us now."

That at least was not a lie.

Brown paused over his writing. Then his tone seemed to soften slightly. "Your grandfather, then. And same goes for your friend here."

"Albert, sir," I said. "Albert Ledbetter."

"Can't Mr. Ledbetter speak for himself?"

Albert answered just above a whisper. "Yes sir. Thank you, sir."

"Save your thank-you's. You won't be thanking anybody by next week. This here ain't no Sunday picnic. Hard, hot labor, low wages, and all for the privilege of being shot at. Think it over carefully. You'll find it much harder getting out of this navy than it was getting in."

Brown sealed the envelope and handed it to me. "Give this to the guard on duty when you come back. He'll get you to the paymaster clerk."

He knocked on the wall next to his desk. Scales appeared again in the doorway.

"See these boys back to the gate," Brown said as we turned to make our escape. "One last thing, Mr. Wood," he called after me. "I deal straight with my men, and I expect the same from them. Try any more tricks and I'll have you horsewhipped."

~

Albert and I left the moored steamer and made our way back through the compound. Without a word the pale young officer once again bounded on ahead and then left us at the gate.

Hector smirked. "Deliver your urgent message?"

I felt a little cockier now, having achieved my aim. "That I did. And you'll be seeing more of us. Albert here and I are signing on the crew tomorrow."

"That so?" said Hector. "How fortunate for you. Hear that, Wallace? New recruits."

Wallace just grinned at us. "Can you bring more licorice?"

~

As we headed back into town Albert and I worked out all the details. So deep were we in discussion that we nearly collided with Nancy Thurman and her younger sister Mary in front of the county library. Nancy was wearing a blue dress, and her blond hair was tied up in a ribbon, ringlets bouncing down her cheeks.

"Hi, Sam," she said and both girls laughed.

Her smile swept every coherent thought from my head. A few paces on I finally summoned the wit to call out "Hello" to her back as they walked down the street, still laughing.

"What was that about?" Albert asked, both curious and impressed. Nancy Thurman had never taken any notice of me before.

"I'm not quite sure," I replied.

But whatever it was, it felt good.

~

That evening when I got home I found the barn door open and the buggy gone. Liz sat in a rocker on the porch, reading a novel.

"Been in any more fights today?" she asked as I climbed up the front steps.

"Not yet," I said.

She leaned back in her chair. "Mary Beth Fox told me that her brother said you took a real mauling from Jack Butler."

"Don't believe everything you hear—especially from Nosy Fox and her half-wit brother."

"Well, I have to get my information from somewhere. *You* never tell me anything."

"Maybe 'cause it ain't your business. Where's the buggy?"

"Grandfather and Martha went to town."

"Why?" I asked.

Liz's eyes widened. "Haven't you heard?"

"No. But I'm sure you'll tell me."

"Justin Pendleton has been killed."

"Killed?"

"Somewhere in Virginia. They got a telegram

today. And what's more—his little brother Tom has run off to join the Confederate Army. The moment he heard the news, he just took off his apron and left the mercantile, straight off to enlist."

I slumped down in the other rocker.

Liz sighed. "Hard to imagine, isn't it? And Justin was the handsome one, too. Grandfather and Martha have gone to call on the Pendletons, to offer condolences. I decided to stay home. It's too sad."

Liz swatted at a fly with her novel, then opened it at her bookmark and began to read again. I sat a moment, going over the news in my head. Justin Pendleton dead, the same smiling young man behind the counter at the mercantile who used to give me hard candy sweets every Saturday morning when I was a kid. The information just wouldn't sink in.

Any doubts I'd had about joining up were now swept away. I rose and went into the house. Grandfather's study was never locked. I slipped inside and left the door ajar. He kept his writing paper in a large oak rolltop desk. I took two sheets in case I made a mistake.

I had just closed the drawer when Liz spoke behind me. "What are you doing?"

I nearly jumped out of my skin. She stood in the open doorway. Normally you can hear Liz anywhere in the house with the *clop-clop* of her block shoe. But when needful, she can move like a cat.

"Nothing," I said.

She raised an eyebrow. "What's that in your hand?"

"Paper. I need it for school."

"Why not just wait and ask for it?"

"Because I need it now."

"I think you're up to something," she said. "Maybe I should tell Grandfather."

I felt as though I could strangle her. She'd ruin everything. "Don't!" I said. "Please. It's important."

"What's important?"

"Just...something about the Academy. You'll find out soon enough. And that's all I'm saying."

That seemed to satisfy her. "Well, you better be real nice to me."

"I'm always nice."

"Ha!" she snorted. "I mean it this time."

"Okay."

I pushed past her and took the writing paper up the stairs to my room and turned the key in the lock. I sat down at my desk and forged the letter. I copied Grandfather's signature from an old banker's note. It didn't make me feel good doing that, but he'd left me no other choice.

Dinner that night was subdued. Neither Martha nor Grandfather said a word the entire meal. Bessie cleared away the dishes and asked, "Does anyone want the last slice of pie?"

"Sure," I said and reached over to take it. But Liz brushed aside my hand, smiling, and kicked me hard under the table. So I pushed the pie plate over to her and asked to be excused.

I found Father's old carpetbag at the back of my

wardrobe. It came to me after his death. He'd used it on his business trips up and down the Mississippi, buying and trading cotton for a commission merchant in New Orleans. That was the last of a string of jobs he'd worked after leaving the navy. Civilian life never suited him. Or that's what Mother used to say when being charitable—those nights he'd return home from Clooney's Tavern, having had a few too many drinks.

I remember one night when I was about six years old, she sent me to fetch him home. I think it was meant to teach him a lesson, to shame him in public. The tavern was loud and smoky and all the men laughed when I appeared at his poker table. But Father just sat me up on his knee as the dealer shuffled the deck for a final hand.

Holding his cards close under my nose he whispered in my ear, his breath stinking of whisky, "We're gonna win this one, Sam."

And he did: a twenty-dollar pot.

Outside the tavern I asked if we were rich now. He laughed and lifted me onto his shoulders. "Richer than Old King Solomon."

All the way home he named the things he'd buy me: a pirate ship, an elephant, a hot air balloon, a harem of Persian slaves, an English castle with thirteen ghosts. But most nights he didn't win, and Mother had to ask Grandfather to clear our bill at the mercantile.

Nothing much was left after Father died, apart from a few items in an old sea chest and that carpetbag, so I was glad to make use of it. I packed three pairs of trousers and matching shirts, collars, ties, an extra jacket, socks, underwear, brush, and comb. Albert and I had agreed that we would be spartan and allow ourselves only one book to keep us occupied in our spare time. I laid out three choices on the bed: *The Selected Works of Shakespeare,* a volume of poetry by Tennyson that I'd won as a prize at school, and my mother's old pocket Bible. The print size in the Shakespeare was far too small, and I had never been much for reading the Bible, so in the end I packed the Tennyson.

Later I went back down to the parlor and found only Martha, sewing by candlelight. Grandfather's chair was empty.

"He's gone off to bed," she said. "It's been a painful day for him. Mr. Pendleton sent us away."

"But they're old friends."

Martha sighed. "Well, he's obviously in shock over Justin. And then there's all that foolish talk about Grandfather going around town."

"Maybe not all that foolish," I muttered, more to myself.

Martha looked up sharply. "Just what do you mean by that?"

"Well, it's easy to be high-minded when it's not your son been killed."

Martha lay down her sewing. "I can't believe I'm hearing this."

My voice rose, as it always did on the defense.

"Nobody asked for this war," I said. "Sitting around and wishing it away doesn't help Henry or any of the other boys out there fighting. Now's the time to stand up and be counted."

Fitzhugh's words again, not mine.

Martha looked dumbfounded. "What you just said—there's so much wrong with it I hardly know where to start."

"Don't bother," I replied, getting up. "I'm going to bed."

Martha said nothing to stop me. I went up to my room and took the carpetbag from the wardrobe. I then slipped down the stairs and out the front door. I hid the bag in the tack room out in the stable. Later, back in my room, I wrote a terse note and put it under my pillow until morning. It read:

Dear Grandfather,

I am sorry if these words cause you pain and disappointment, but I have decided not to wait any longer in joining the Southern Cause. I know you do not agree but I feel it is my Duty and that of the family to aid in the Defense of our land against the Invading Enemy. Please pray for me as I will for you, and Martha and Liz.

Love,
Sam

I knew as I wrote them that the words were hollow, acknowledging nothing, and I was sorry that my actions would break my grandfather's heart. But to say more might have caused me to doubt my resolve. Besides, it was late, and I had too much else to think about.

~

Next morning I awoke before daylight. The house was dark and still. I dressed quietly and sneaked downstairs to the kitchen. On the breakfast table I left a note saying I'd gone early to school. That meant nobody would find the other letter, the one I'd left in my room on my desk, until probably dinnertime. I slipped out the back door and retrieved my bag from the tack room in the stable.

Dawn had broken in a clear, cloudless sky. I had one stop to make before meeting up with Albert. I set off across the peach orchard. Low sunlight filtered through the trees and seemed to pick out every branch and twig, every mote of dandelion fluff, every insect, every sparrow. It was as if I'd never really noticed these things before; all seemed to take on an exaggerated significance.

A dark grove of tall cedars lay on the far side of the orchard. Thirty years ago my mother's younger brother Stephen died at age ten in an influenza outbreak, and Grandfather had cleared a burial ground for him there within the grove. Granny Toynbee was buried there, along with my parents. Both of their gravestones bear the same year: 1856.

Mother lived only a month after Doctor Mason

diagnosed the cancer in her belly. He made an appointment for her to meet a surgeon in Jackson, but she refused to make the trip. She said that God would look after her one way or another. Nobody expected her to go so quickly, least of all Father. And in no time he was gone, too.

A few months after Mother's funeral, he boarded a river steamer down to New Orleans. He got drunk in the saloon and lost at cards as usual, then left the poker table in a temper. The steward on the boat said his bed had not been slept in that night. A farmer found his body washed up against the levee just north of Vidalia. Nobody could say whether it was an accident or not. He left no note. All they found in his pocket was an old letter from my mother written to him when he was a midshipman in the navy.

So the three of us kids had to leave our house in town and move to Grandfather's farm at Sandhill. As if by a sudden violent storm, almost everything we'd known had been swept away.

That morning I noticed someone had visited the grove recently, probably the day before. On each grave lay a bunch of wild roses bound with daisy stems. Most likely this was Liz. Even as a child she'd often come here to play, perfectly at home among the gravestones. Martha, too, sometimes brought her book and sat on the small bench Cope had hewn from one of the fallen cedars. But I'd always avoided the place. I found no comfort there, only painful memories. I still felt love for my parents, ached with the loss. But over time the constant wear of grief had dulled my feeling, as if a callus had formed over my soul.

I'm not sure why I felt I had to visit the grove that morning. Can you really feel the presence of loved ones at their graves? Or does being there just make you more aware of their absence? Was I looking for my parents' blessing, their approval? Maybe if they'd still been alive they would have tried to stop me going, like Grandfather. I'd only known them as a child; now I was nearly a man. I had little to go on. Father had been a soldier, so maybe he would have understood. With Mother, I wasn't so sure.

I picked up my bag; a breeze stirred the high branches. I felt I should say something like people do in books: tearful oaths, solemn promises. But the words that came to mind just seemed foolish.

So I whispered, "I'm going now."

Then I turned and cut into the deep woods to pick up the Benton road down the hill.

~

Albert lived in town and I'd arranged to meet him that morning by the pump at the end of his street. But when I arrived I found Mr. Ledbetter waiting instead. He looked grim.

"Come on with me, Sam."

Albert had been undecided whether he would also forge a letter or raise the question of enlisting with his father. I favored the first choice. But whatever he'd decided, the situation didn't look good.

I followed Mr. Ledbetter into the house. He stood well over six feet, thin and balding. He worked for the Yazoo County clerk of court, keeping records. Albert's father was a quiet man, not that he had much choice in the matter, being married to Mrs. Ledbetter.

He led me to the parlor. There Albert stood next to his mother, who sat on a chaise longue still in her dressing gown. A packed canvas bag rested at Albert's feet. Both looked tearful.

Mr. Ledbetter took a key from his waistcoat pocket and opened a panel in a large oak bureau. He took out a bottle of Kentucky rye whisky and filled three shot glasses.

"Come here, boys," he said, and handed us each a glass. "I'm proud of you both. Take care of each other."

He drank his measure in one swallow. I took a sip, my first taste of whisky. It seared down my throat and I tried not to retch. Albert choked on his and began to cough. Mr. Ledbetter embraced him and gently patted his back, as though burping an infant.

"You be smart," he whispered. "Come back home to us."

Albert pushed gently away from his father and turned to Mrs. Ledbetter.

"Good-bye, Mother."

She looked down at her slippers. "Go on now, enough of this nonsense. Keep away from card games and liquor," she said, shooting a hot glance at Mr. Ledbetter. "Don't take up cursing or any other rude soldier habits. And remember to say your prayers. Go now before I start..."

Her face seemed to crumple. Albert picked up his bag and touched her bowed head and then we left. Five or ten minutes we walked in silence. I could feel the doubt, the hesitation in his step. But I was his best friend. I suppose he would've followed me anywhere.

Just as we crossed Main Street and headed down toward the river, I reached into my bag and pulled out the volume of Tennyson. "So what did you choose?"

Albert gave a sheepish grin and dug into his canvas satchel. He pulled out a slim book entitled *Principles and Practice in Integral Calculus.* I shook my head.

"You are one pathetic soul."

4

I expected a hard time from Hector when we returned to the gate that morning, but he and Wallace weren't on guard duty. Another soldier took the note that Captain Brown had written and without question escorted us to the paymaster's office on the *Capitol*. It was a small, airless room dominated by an enormous desk. Behind it sat a pale, flabby officer in an ill-fitting uniform. Albert and I hesitated in the doorway.

"Well, come on in," he barked. "Don't have all morning."

I handed him the note and our letters of permission. The officer gave them a quick glance and grunted, pulling out two sets of enlistment papers. He recorded all our details: full name, age, height, weight, education, religion, scars or other distinguishing features, next of kin. He then laid the completed forms in front of us.

"All right, gentlemen. Here's the deal. Enlistment

period, one year. Rating, Boy. Pay, twelve dollars a month. Need your signatures at the X."

And we signed, easy as that. He stamped the forms and scrawled out a note.

"Congratulations. You're in Jeff Davis's navy. Take this and go find Quartermaster Eagan. You'll probably hear him before you see him."

"Thank you, sir," I said, and then stammered. "It's...it's an honor to serve."

"Fine," said the officer, having already picked up another file. "Close the door on your way out."

Heading back down the hallway to the stairs, Albert and I grinned at each other. It had been just too simple.

We wandered back out into the shipyard. A hot mid-morning sun beat down, and I began to sweat under my Sunday suit. The compound buzzed with activity. The steam-driven crane on the *Capitol* hoisted a segment of rail iron aloft and over to the front gun shield of the *Arkansas*. Workmen swung it into place, careful to avoid getting their fingers crushed. A soldier struggled past us toting a bucket of iron bolts. I asked if he could direct us to Quartermaster Eagan. He pointed to a large camp tent with a wide front awning under which two men leaned over a trestle table, looking at plans. One wore civilian dress, the other a dusty blue naval jacket and gray trousers. Both looked hot and annoyed and were deep in argument.

"Well, it won't be you swallowing grape shot when

the damn thing jams open!" shouted the uniformed man, whom I took to be Eagan.

"Not a problem. We'll tool down the pins."

"Just get it working. Now the block and tackle—" Eagan looked up as we approached. "Damnation! What now?"

I began to answer but he raised one finger to stop me.

"No. Wait over by the river until I call you." And he turned back to his plans. "Block and tackle...."

~

Albert and I waited over half an hour sitting in the burnt grass on the riverbank. It promised to be a scorching day. A boy about our age passed a few times carrying a water bucket and ladle. He was French by the look of him, small with dark eyes and curly brown hair, and fine features almost like a girl's. I was desperate for a drink. But the boy offered nothing but dirty looks.

Eagan finished his business and shouted to us. "You two. Over here."

We jogged to the tent and I handed him the note. His eyes skimmed over it, and he pulled out a silver pocket watch and checked the time.

"Okay. Follow me."

Eagan led us back over the gangplank to the *Capitol*. Most of the crew and workmen were being quartered onboard until the *Arkansas* was battle ready.

The quartermaster, a lean leathery man with close-cropped hair, moved with swift impatience. His face was clean shaven; a thick raised scar branched across one cheek from ear to mouth. I later heard the rumor that a 32-pounder had exploded in his face at Vera Cruz. Nobody knew for sure; nobody dared ask. But it was terrible to behold, that scar, especially when Eagan got angry.

He led us to a cramped cabin on the main deck. It had three wooden berths up the two side walls and a small grimy window in between. Three of the bunks were already taken.

"Find a free berth and stow your gear." Eagan looked down at my swollen carpetbag. "Think you're on holiday, boy? What you got in there?"

"Spare clothes mainly, sir."

Eagan shook his head. "You from the town?"

"Yes sir," I replied.

"Schoolboys?"

"Yes sir."

He frowned. "God help us."

I put my bag on the lowest bunk and Albert chose the same one opposite. Eagan turned to go.

"Change out of them fancy duds and put on some work clothes. Meet me back where you found me in five minutes. And I do mean five."

He left the cabin. Albert pulled open his smaller bag.

"Don't we get uniforms?" he asked.

"Maybe later," I said. "Better get moving."

THE PASSAGE

I changed clothes quickly, but Albert broke a lace tying his boot and struggled to rethread the frayed end. I told him to hurry but it was no use.

We arrived back at the tent at a trot and found Eagan staring down at his watch. The scar on his cheek stood out bloodless and white. He snapped shut the case and slipped it back into his vest pocket, and in the same motion struck me hard across the cheek with the back of his hand. It stung like fury, and tears sprang to my eyes at the shock and shame of it.

"Never keep me waiting." He shoved a straw planter's hat on his head and made off toward the river. "Come on," he said.

Albert glanced at me, eyes wide. I brushed away the tears and pushed past him. Eagan led us down the bank and shouted at two boys scrubbing clothes at the water's edge:

"Conroys!"

Both looked up from the barrel and washboard. They were identical twins, with thick black hair and pale, freckled skin burnt red by the sun.

"Come here. Where's Autin?"

"Over there, sir," said one of the twins. He pointed to the stern of the *Capitol* where the boy who'd been carrying the water bucket now sat peeling potatoes. "Autin!" Eagan hollered. "Double quick."

The boy leapt to his feet and bounced over the gangplank to shore. Eagan waited as he jogged down the bank.

"Want you to meet your new bunk mates: Wood

and Ledbetter. I expect you to keep 'em straight. Understood, Autin?"

The boy smirked. "Yes sir. My pleasure."

"Your pleasure's got nothing to do with it," said Eagan.

One of the twins began to laugh. His brother elbowed him hard in the ribs. Eagan glared and continued, "Autin here's an old tar, practically born on the river. So you follow his lead, less'n that's into trouble. Cause you don't want trouble with me."

Autin grinned down at his boots. Eagan ignored him.

"You may have noticed the haste with which this boatyard is operating. Not four days' sailing from here lies the entire Union river fleet under the command of our formerly esteemed Admiral Farragut. And the Yazoo is dropping fast. This ship here has to be battle ready in four weeks or we'll be stranded up river, no more of a threat to the Yankees than two rats in a rowboat."

Eagan then turned on his heel and snapped, "That's introductions over. Back to work. You two follow me."

He led us to one of the equipment sheds near the gate. Inside he found two spades and tossed them at us. Albert dropped his with a clatter.

Eagan sighed and then headed off toward the far end of the compound. We trailed after him.

Captain Brown had requisitioned all of Yazoo Shipwrights with outbuildings and other facilities.

Among these was a stinking four-seater privy in one corner of the boatyard. Just nearing it made me gag. It was here that Albert and I undertook our first official duty in the Confederate Navy.

Eagan shoved open the door to the privy. A cloud of black flies rose from every surface. The stench was beyond belief.

"Upwards of two hundred men working on this site and all of them doing their business in that pit," he said, and kicked open one of the seat covers.

More flies swarmed out the four dark holes, which hummed with maggots.

"Take a look. It's filled to the brim."

Both Albert and I backed away. Eagan laughed and led us around to the rear of the shack where another man stood holding a shovel in a trench about knee deep. He was stripped to the waist, thin and bony, dark sun-browned skin streaked with sweat and dirt. Eagan stood at the edge of the trench.

"That all you done in two hours digging, Collins?"

"Hard going in this clay, sir."

"Well, I've brought you some help. You two boys do what Collins here tells you. Never was a man more fit to dig a ditch."

Eagan then left us to it. I climbed down into the trench with the spade. The morning had certainly not turned out as expected.

"So where do we start?" I asked.

Collins planted his shovel in the hard clay. "Just start digging. Ain't college physics."

~

The sun bore down on the unshaded spot with no hint of a breeze. Flies and gnats from the tall grass clouded over us, crawling into our eyes and up our noses, making it hard to breathe. Collins hadn't exaggerated about the digging. Loose topsoil gave way to thick damp clay that clung to the shovel blade. The muscles in my back and arms soon burned with exhaustion. Albert worked silently beside me, taking air in gulps, his skin blotchy with insect bites.

Collins said nothing as he dug, slow and steady. A hard-worn man, impossible to age, eyes sunken and bloodshot, skin stretched tight over his skull. I noticed a tremor in his hand each time he paused to brush away the flies. We later learned that he had once been an officer in the old Federal Navy but had been busted down to ordinary seaman for drunkenness and dereliction of duty.

The morning grew ever hotter as the sun climbed the sky. I'd left my watch back on the boat and had no idea of the time. Autin finally arrived with his water bucket. It must have been nearly noon.

Collins scowled. "Where you been?"

Autin shrugged. "Here and there. You need a drink, Frank? Sorry, I only got water." He laughed and dipped his ladle and handed it down to Collins, who swallowed the water in a single gulp. "Looks like thirsty work. Want another sip?"

Collins shook his head. "Better see to these boys."

Autin acted as though he'd only just noticed us. He swirled the ladle in his bucket. By then Albert was not looking so good. He'd dropped his shovel and sat slumped on the edge of the trench. Autin filled the ladle and offered it to me first. I should have passed it to Albert. He looked more in need. But never in my life had I felt such a thirst. I seemed to lack the power of choice. I grabbed the ladle and sucked the water down, nearly choking.

"Not so fast, chief," said Autin. "Puke it up and you ain't getting no more."

I handed back the ladle.

Autin swirled it in the bucket again, spilling water into the dirt. "Nice hole. I'm impressed. Guess you boys didn't figure on this; thought you'd just change out them fancy clothes right into a nice uniform. Start marching round the place, playing at sailors. Not digging no crap pit."

"Shut up, Jordi," Collins snapped, "and get that boy over there some water."

Albert sat still slumped in exhaustion.

Autin dunked the ladle again. "Sorry, chief." He held it out. "You thirsty?"

Just as he spoke Albert toppled sideways and rolled into the pit unconscious.

Collins jumped up. "Dammit, Jordi. Gimme that bucket." He snatched it away from Autin, knelt down beside Albert, and rolled him onto his back. He pulled a neckerchief from his back pocket and dunked it in the water, then wrung it over Albert's forehead.

Eagan arrived. "What's the problem?"

"Boy's gone with the heat, sir."

Eagan cursed and jumped down into the trench. "Okay. Let's get him to the river before his brains boil."

The quartermaster lifted Albert up under his arms, and Collins and I each took a leg. Autin didn't look so cocky now.

"Bring that bucket!" Eagan shouted at him. "You been watering these men?"

"Yes sir. Just now."

"Just now? It's past noon, you son of a whore. Was this deliberate?"

"No sir."

"Well, guess what, Autin? Deliberate or not, you just earned the afternoon shovel shift."

~

We carried Albert to a sandy bank downriver. Here the men came in the evenings to swim and bathe. We laid him down in the shallows, and I held his head above the surface while Collins splashed water into his face. He soon came to and asked for a drink. Autin handed me a ladleful, which Albert drank and then immediately threw up.

"Not so much at once," Eagan snapped.

A few minutes later Albert was sitting up, taking small sips of water.

Eagan looked again at his watch and turned to leave. "Hope you two ain't gonna be more trouble than you're worth. Soon as he's recovered, both of you report to Cook for mess duty."

Autin shot me a hot glance as he and Collins headed back to the trench. Albert looked up after they'd left. "What happened?"

"Well," I said, "it was so hot that kindly Mr. Eagan decided we should all go for a swim."

But Albert didn't laugh.

~

Ten minutes we sat on the riverbank in the shade of a large willow. Neither of us spoke, but I'm sure we shared the same thought: home. Just one morning and I already longed to be away from that place, to be back at Sandhill, sitting on the porch reading a novel, with the expectation of lunch soon on the table. Even Liz's incessant chatter would be welcome.

Maybe we could return to the paymaster's office. Ask for our papers back, give him some excuse. But what? I was too beat to think. Soon Eagan would return and shout at us for shirking. We had to move.

"Come on," I urged. "Better report to the cook like he said."

I gave Albert a hand up. He looked shaky on his feet. Neither of us had eaten all day. If there had been a noon meal, we must have missed it. We crossed the gangplank to the *Capitol* and made our way to the galley.

Chief cook for the *Arkansas* was a burly Irishman named Jake Bixby from the wharf district of New

Orleans. That afternoon we found him at his butcher's block, cleaver in hand, chopping beef for the evening stew. He stood there in his bloody apron, blue bandana tied round his head. He had bushy dark sideburns and a perfectly trimmed and waxed handlebar mustache. His cheeks glowed beet-red with the heat of the bread ovens; his smile was jovial, but his eyes as black as coal.

"So what have we here?" he sang in a deep baritone voice as he planted the blade of his cleaver into the wooden block. "You must be the two young gentlemen of whom Autin has spoken so highly. Let's have your names."

I introduced us. Bixby shook both our hands and then gestured to another man, heavy-set with a badly pox-scarred face, who was chopping vegetables. "Wilson here is Cook's mate. He's rather ill-tempered today. Got a rotten tooth."

Wilson nodded to us, unsmiling.

Bixby winked. "So how are you finding the sailor's life so far?"

"Not exactly what we expected," I replied.

"Eagan working you hard? Just got to hold fast. Nothing lower in this navy than a boy, excepting maybe a nigger."

I was uncertain if this was an insult or an observation. But the man seemed friendly enough, so I saw no harm in asking. "Do you think we could maybe get a bite to eat? We seemed to have missed the noon meal, and neither of us had any breakfast this morning."

Wilson turned to us with a crooked smile and then

glanced over at Bixby. Nothing obvious seemed to change in the cook's manner—just white teeth glinting under his mustache as he grinned.

"Well, of course. What can I get for you boys? I'm here to please. How about some of the court bouillon to start, or maybe oysters on the half shell?"

Bixby's voice rose in volume and pitch and he wrenched loose his cleaver.

"And then what? Filet mignon, suckling pig, pan-fried mullet, and sparrow tongues simmered in butter and garlic? That take your fancy?"

The cook raised his cleaver and swung it down hard and clean through a thick joint of beef. Wilson sniggered but then grabbed his cheek in pain.

"Sorry, boys. I kid you. I am a kidder. No food except at mealtimes. But I tell you what. You can chew on a raw potato while you finish peeling that lot."

A large burlap sack of potatoes sat near the doorway. And that's how Albert and I spent most of the afternoon, peeling the potatoes and tossing them into a large pot of water. Near mealtime we were sent to fetch coal to bank the stoves, and to bring fresh water from the boatyard pump.

Autin appeared in the galley just before the dinner bell. His clothes were filthy, his face smeared with clay. He looked exhausted.

"Where in hell you been?" Bixby snapped. "Left more than half them potatoes unpeeled."

Autin sighed.

"Eagan—"

But Bixby cut him off. "Spare me the details. Just

get cleaned up and into your whites. You're on officers' mess tonight."

Wilson rang a brass bell, and men—sailors, soldiers, and civilian workers—began to fill the dining saloon, shouting and laughing. Some had just finished shifts; others were just starting. Captain Brown had teams working twenty-four hours a day to get the *Arkansas* finished. At night the site was lit with torches and pine knots.

Albert and I carried steaming pots of potato mash and beef stew to the serving tables where Wilson dished out. I was starved by then but dared not touch anything until Bixby said. Next we cleared the tin plates from the table and washed them in tubs filled with scalding hot water. Only after we had all the pots, pans, dishes, and utensils dried and stowed did Bixby let us sit out with plates of leftover stew and potatoes. I wolfed mine down but Albert hardly ate a thing.

"What's wrong?" I asked him.

"I'm too tired to eat," he said, looking gray and exhausted.

"Better at least try," I said.

But he only picked at his food.

It was after dark before we made it back to our cabin. The Conroy twins sat on the floor playing cards, and Autin lay up on his bunk reading an old newspaper. Albert collapsed onto his unmade mattress without a word and fell asleep still in his work clothes.

"Tuckered out?" asked one of the twins.

"Yeah," I replied, stripping off my damp shirt. "Been a hard day."

The boy lay down his card hand. "I'm Peter, by the way, and this here's my ugly brother Simon."

I shook hands with both and then immediately forgot who was which. Later I came to know Simon as slightly thicker about the nose (broken at age seven by his brother), and Peter by a small mole under his chin and a tendency to laugh at anything remotely funny. They hailed from New Madrid, Missouri, though both had been born in County Cork, Ireland, in a family of eight. Two of the older Conroy brothers also served on the crew and were veterans of the riverboat battles at Island No. 10. Simon-Peter (as Autin called them) ran away from home to follow their brothers to Yazoo City and the *Arkansas*.

"My brother Dermot wanted to kill us when we turned up here," said Peter. "Heck of a long way from New Madrid. We had to steal Hiram Figg's skiff and row out to the *Crystal City*. Slipped aboard while the night watchman was snoozing. We rode her all the way to Vicksburg, hiding under the canvas in one of the lifeboats. Like to've died with the heat and him over there farting."

"Weren't me," said Simon. "You're the one ate all the beans."

"That's a lie," Peter said.

"You're the liar."

"Trust me," said Peter. "That boy'd gag a maggot. Ask Autin."

But Autin just ducked behind his paper.

"You're always blaming me," said Simon. "Most times it's you doing the farting."

"Stinking windbag," Peter muttered.

"Don't you call me that!"

"Windbag."

And so it went, until before I knew it Simon leaned over and threw a vicious punch that knocked Peter back against one of the bunks. His playing cards scattered across the floor. Peter leapt up, nose bleeding, and slammed a knee into his brother's face. Both then tumbled across the floor, punching and gouging. Autin dropped his paper and jumped down from his bunk.

"Damn you two. Cut it out. Remember what Eagan said."

He then grabbed the shirt of whoever was on top and yanked him away. "Don't just stand there," he snapped at me over his shoulder.

I grabbed the other twin.

Both strained to get at each other, pale faces crimson with rage.

"Better call somebody," I said. "They'll kill each other."

Autin shook his head. "Naw. It happens all the time."

Just then we heard voices approaching. Autin pulled Simon to his feet. I stooped to gather up the cards. Peter pinched his nose to stop the blood.

Captain Brown and two other officers appeared in the cabin doorway. Autin and the twins jumped to attention and I followed suit. Albert slept on. I reached down and tugged at his leg.

"That's okay. Leave him be," said Brown. "I see you decided to join us, Mr. Wood. So how are you settling in?"

"Fine. Thank you, sir."

"Look's like Eagan's working you hard enough, judging by the state of your friend here."

"Yes sir."

Brown turned to the other officers. "I served with this boy's father on my first commission as lieutenant at Vera Cruz. He was one hell of a gun captain."

Brown gave me a hard look, just for an instant, as though seeking some trace of my father in me. I felt my face redden.

"These are two of my officers," he said. "Lieutenant Read and Lieutenant Gift. Read here is local to Yazoo County."

The officer reached out to shake my hand, a small man in his early twenties with long brown hair, dark eyes, and an easy smile. "I do believe I've met your sister Martha, at a cotillion down near Dover last Christmas. She still engaged to that bookish fellow?"

"Yes sir. Henry Brooks. He's serving with the Confederate Corps of Engineers in Mobile."

Read's eyes widened. "Mobile, eh? Guess he don't get home much."

Gift shook his head, a dour-looking man also in his twenties, tall and fair with pale blue eyes. "I'd keep my sister well clear of him if I were you."

Read grinned and then noticed the book sitting on top of my bunk. He picked it up and read the spine.

"I'll tell you, it's gonna take some getting used to this new navy. Boy ratings who read Tennyson. How does that poem go? 'Half a league, half a league, half a league onward…into the valley of death rode the six hundred…' That right, Wood?"

"Yes sir—something like that."

Gift snorted.

Read turned to him. "You ever read Tennyson?" he asked.

"Nope."

"You ever read anything apart from ordinance manuals?"

"Not if I can help it."

"Well, Gift, you need to broaden your horizons. Stirring stuff, this." Read gave me back the book.

Brown looked down at his watch. "You boys stow them cards and get some rest."

When they left the cabin, Autin climbed back up into his bunk. "Say, you're pretty well connected, ain't you, chief?" he said. "Too bad that don't mean crap to Eagan."

He laughed and went back to his paper.

After lights-out I lay in my bunk, already dreading the morning. I tried to convince myself things would get better now that we knew what to expect, just like the first day in a new class at school. But I knew this was a vain hope. I thought about Grandfather getting my letter, Martha crying, maybe even Liz. Would he come for me? Did I want him to? One of the twins began to snore loudly, but even so, sleep came, swift and deep.

5

I was awakened that next morning before dawn by a bright light shining in my eyes. I sat up in fright, slamming my head on the bunk above. Bixby held a lantern to my face. It took a moment to remember where I was.

"Come on, princess. Wake up. Mess duty. You too, boyo."

I heard Albert groan.

Bixby raised his lantern to Autin's bunk. "Get your sorry ass out of that sack."

Autin muttered something and rolled his face to the wall. Bixby reached up and slapped him hard on the back of the head.

"Now!"

"Okay! I'm gettin'." Autin sat up.

Bixby turned for the door. "Five minutes."

Autin cursed and struck a match. He lit a candle and yawned. "And I was having me a fine dream too, certain gal I know in the French Quarter."

It sounded like bluster but I didn't say anything. I

sat up and pulled on my trousers. Every muscle in my body ached with the effort. Albert lay on his bunk unmoving. He still wore the same clothes from the day before.

"Hey, beanpole," Autin said. "Best get a move on. You don't want to mess with Jake, especially not in the morning."

I tugged at his arm. "Come on, Albert." But he didn't budge. I knelt down next to him. "Sorry," I whispered. "I got us into this."

Autin was grinning.

Albert rose up onto his elbow with a groan. "It's okay. I'm just waking up."

We washed our faces at the stern with a bucket of river water. The sun had yet to rise, and we could see the glow of the forges down the bank and men working by lantern light inside the gun deck of the *Arkansas*.

Bixby was in a foul mood. We soon learned that he was like that most mornings before his first belt of whisky. No jovial banter, just barked commands punctuated with savage cursing directed at the slightest mistake. Most of this abuse he poured on Autin, who took it without reply.

We prepared breakfast for the hundred or so men changing shifts. I fetched buckets of water from the pump for coffee and hominy grits, and more coal for the stoves. Albert chopped up leftover potatoes for hash browns. Wilson cracked eggs at a rate of two a second (one in each hand) for scramble while Bixby grilled slabs of bacon.

Heat and steam from the stoves made the air hardly breathable. The abuse from Bixby got worse as time neared for the breakfast bell.

"Hey, Wilson! You making scramble or India rubber? That mess ain't fit to eat. Toast! Damn you Autin, you gutter-bred mongrel. Burn it again like last week and I'll rip your ears off."

Just as Bixby reached for the bell, Albert went to move one of the coffeepots off the boil, not noticing that the handle nearly glowed with heat. He howled in agony and toppled the pot over the stove in an explosion of steam. Bixby went wild. Nose to nose with Albert, he cursed and spat, calling upon mothers and dogs and bishops and broomsticks. It was almost poetic. Albert stood frozen to the spot, face pinched as though braced against a fierce wind. And like a whirlwind it was over and forgotten in seconds, at least by Bixby. He yanked the bell rope and men poured into the hall.

Autin balanced two large trays and headed up to the officers' mess. Albert and I carried out the serving pots to Wilson, who spooned out the portions. I spotted Hector and Wallace in the chow line. Hector brushed back his greasy hair and smiled at my apron. He then snapped his heels in mock salute.

Wallace offered a toothless grin and asked, "Brung any licorice?"

Around nine we finished washing and racking all the breakfast dishes and pots and pans, and went out on the stern deck for a breather. It was another cloudless day, already getting hot. But just as we sat down to eat some breakfast, Eagan appeared on the bank and shouted to us.

"You boys got a job to finish! Go fetch Autin and meet me at the equipment store."

But Autin was not in the galley. Albert went to look for him in the cabin while I searched the rest of the *Capitol*. I found him up on the top deck. He sat on an upturned pail, hunched over the same old newspaper. Steam was up in the engines, and the drilling machinery rattled and whined loudly such that Autin couldn't hear me approach. He held the broken end of a pencil and had made dozens of little marks down the columns of the front page. I touched him on the shoulder and he jumped.

"What're you doing, sneaking up on me?" He quickly folded away the paper.

"I wasn't sneaking. Eagan wants us."

"Eagan? Ah hell. What for?"

"He wasn't specific," I said. "Better hurry though."

~

Eagan waited by the supply shed with the silver watch in hand. He snapped it shut as we approached. I held back, expecting another slap, but he turned without comment and went inside. This time he fetched out two shovels, four fire buckets, a claw hammer, and a coil of rope. We then followed him with the gear back toward the privy.

Autin muttered, "I got a bad feeling about this."

Collins was already in the trench digging with his spade. He and Autin had made surprising progress in a single afternoon. It now measured around four by ten feet, and was nearly four feet deep.

Eagan nodded. "That'll suffice, Collins. Now, gentlemen. We got a dilemma here. As you can tell, our privy is too full. So what do we do—move the privy or move its contents? Seeing as we're in the business of building a warship and not a crap house, I'm afraid it has to be the latter option. So let's get started."

Eagan directed Collins to use the claw hammer to pry off the four-seater wooden bench inside the privy. He retched as he pulled out the plank.

The quartermaster then held a handkerchief to his nose and cursed. "Okay now," he said. "Get on in there with them buckets. Faster you get to it, quicker it'll be done."

Flies swarmed in and out the doorway. Nobody wanted to go first. Collins coughed and spat and then tied a neckerchief over this mouth and nose. He picked up his bucket and went inside. We had to follow. Words cannot do justice to the stench of that place. A wriggling skein of maggots covered the surface of the open pit. I watched as Collins scooped up the first bucketful, eyes pinched with tears. I leaned over the edge with my face turned aside and did the same. Outside again I managed to reach the trench and dump the contents before losing my breakfast.

Eagan stood over me as I dry heaved. "Probably better off with an empty stomach," he said.

Just then I turned to see Autin on his knees doing the same. Only Albert avoided being sick and that was just because he'd hardly touched his breakfast. I watched him carry his bucket in a daze, the contents slopping onto his shoes and trouser legs.

"Hey, boy!" Eagan shouted. "You sleepwalking? Take more care."

All that morning under a fierce sun we emptied the latrine, bucket by bucket, using ropes when the level dropped too low to reach. Filth covered my hands and arms, soaked my trousers, splattered my face and hair.

Near noontime we had the pit about half empty. We were all sick and beat, but Albert looked the worst, toiling just to move one foot forward the other.

I had just hoisted up a bucket-load inside the privy when I heard Albert scream. I dashed outside to find him wallowing in sludge at the bottom of the trench. He'd gone to dump his bucket, and the ground at the edge had given way under his feet. Autin looked on in horror.

I ran to the edge and held out my arm. He was hollering, covered in brown muck from head to toe. He took my hand, but his feet kept slipping on the slick clay sides. Collins lent an arm and together we managed to hoist him out. Albert crawled away across the grass, weeping now, great gulping sobs like a child.

"Come on, son," Collins said. "I know it's awful, but pull yourself together. Go on down to the river and get washed. Better hurry before Eagan comes back."

So I walked him over to the Yazoo. Tears and snot streaked down the filth on his face.

"I can't do this anymore," he moaned. "I need to go home."

"But we signed papers," I said. "We'd be deserters. They could shoot us." He looked so miserable, I added, "Maybe we should run away. Go to Mexico or Brazil."

But Albert seemed not to hear. He just kept saying the same thing over again.

"I can't do this. I can't do this."

~

A group of off-duty soldiers were bathing along the riverbank. They hooted and hollered and pinched their noses as we walked on downstream. Albert dove into the water and came up scrubbing at his face. He tore off his shirt and trousers and tried to rinse them out. Just then Eagan appeared on the bank.

"What is this?"

I tried to explain but he wasn't interested.

"Ledbetter. Put your clothes back on and get back to work." He then turned to me. "Go get cleaned up. Captain Brown wants to see you."

Albert looked up at me in panic.

"It's okay," I whispered. "I'll be back soon."

"Move it, Wood!" Eagan snarled.

I turned and jogged away up the bank without looking back.

~

On the *Capitol* I pulled off my filthy clothes and washed myself the best I could with a bucket. I then put on my suit trousers and a clean shirt.

"Come," Lieutenant Brown called when I knocked at his door.

He sat behind his desk, and in his hand was my permission letter to enlist. Grandfather sat in a hard wooden chair opposite him. I nearly choked.

"Can you explain this, Mr. Wood?"

But the words would not come.

"No sir," I finally managed.

Fearful as I was at having been caught out, it was good to see Grandfather. He looked older somehow, tired and pained.

Brown leaned back in his chair. "I do understand the urge behind your actions. But this is forgery."

He slipped the letter back into his desk drawer. "So what am I to do? Your grandfather here tells me that you're a confused young man. That you misunderstand what it is we're fighting for here. That to you this is just some sort of game. That so, Wood?"

"No sir."

"The good reverend here has also threatened to contact the Navy Department in Richmond. Make all kinds of trouble for me. Enlisting a minor without valid permission from a guardian. Now, trouble I can handle. What I want to know—is it worth it? So I put it to you, Mr. Samuel Wood Junior. Do you want to go home now, or stay on my crew? Make a choice."

Grandfather stared in silence down at his hands resting his lap. I had to choose, standing right there in front of him. One word and I could be riding home again in the buggy to a nice meal and quiet room with no shouts, no threats, no latrine duty.

Of course, the deal didn't include Albert. The permission letter from his father was genuine. And I was the reason he'd joined up. Could I really desert him just like that? Could I go back to Yazoo Academy and be taunted as a milksop and a coward?

It seemed I had no real choice. "May I stay, sir?"

Brown gave me a long, hard look and then replied, "You may indeed."

He then turned to Grandfather. "Got your answer, Reverend?"

Grandfather sighed and rose from the chair.

Tears burned my eyes. I could so easily have gone home with him. "I'm sorry," I said. "But don't you see, I have to stay now."

Brown stood up from his desk. "That'll be all, Wood."

Grandfather reached out for my shoulders and pulled me into a stiff embrace. "It's okay, Sam," he whispered and held me tight. "I can't make your choices for you. Not any more. Just take care and come home soon."

Brown opened his office door. "Go on now, back to your duties."

~

Down at the trench the latrine squad sat having a breather. I was back in my work clothes again. It'd been torture exchanging the clean shirt and trousers for the stinking rags I'd left hung over the railing.

Autin snorted, "Word from Eagan was that your grandpappy come to fetch you home. So what are you doing back here?"

I sat next to them in the grass. "What? And let y'all steal my fun?"

Collins laughed. Autin shook his head in disbelief.

And Albert smiled for the first time that long tiring day.

6

It was a week or so later when I first heard the guns. Just after dark I'd come out from the galley to dump a pot of greasy water over the stern. A warm breeze blew out of the west carrying a faint rumble, like the sound of an approaching thunderstorm. I paused to listen and noticed the glowing tip of a cigar on the deck above.

"Evening, Wood."

It was Lieutenant Read. I stiffened and saluted, still holding my pot.

There was another rumble, and Read leaned out over the railing. "So what do you make of that?"

"Sounds like a storm coming," I replied.

He shook his head. "That ain't no storm. That's Vicksburg. Some of Farragut's gunboats taking ranges. Just like in April down at the Passes below New Orleans. What you're hearing is a 7-ton mortar mounted on a schooner; looks a bit like a giant kettle. Lobs a 200-pound shell in a high trajectory and drops it straight through the roof."

"Are they shelling the town?" I asked Read.

"Not on purpose. They'll be aiming for the river batteries, our heavy guns. Knock them out and they own the river. But it's not exactly a precise business, naval bombardment. You'll get a few stray shells."

I found it hard to imagine. Just last October I went to Vicksburg with Grandfather on church business. I spent the afternoon wandering the town, from the wharves along the river up to the grand mansions and churches high on the bluff. People crowded the steep streets, in and out of the busy shops: drug stores, bakeries, jewelers, gunsmiths, dry goods, boot makers, butchers, ironmongers. I remembered sitting on the steps of the new courthouse eating a penny loaf of gingerbread and enjoying the bustle. I couldn't imagine that place now under bombardment.

Read took a long pull on his cigar. "So Wood, I hear you want a navy career..."

So much for the imperiled populace of Vicksburg.

"Yes sir," I said, not exactly acknowledging to myself the lie, though feeling it wriggle under my skin.

"Bad timing with a war on. How's that for irony?" He let out a laugh, oddly high, almost girlish. "No doubt Richmond will open a Confederate naval academy some day soon. Or maybe the North'll sue for peace and then you can apply at Annapolis. I'd be happy to write a letter on your behalf."

"Thank you, sir."

"We got to stick together, us Yazoo County boys.

Jeff Davis himself wrote a letter for me as a favor to my uncle. That's how I got in. It's all who you know."

Again from the west came the thunder of naval guns. Read looked wistfully downriver. He then flicked the glowing end of his cigar in a high arc out over the dark water and bid me good night. I felt myself shiver. Was it with excitement, fear, dread? Maybe one, maybe all.

~

Over those long first days at the naval yard we settled into a routine of sorts. Mealtimes belonged to Bixby: peel and chop, wash and scour. Quartermaster Eagan had us for the other hours: scrubbing the decks of the *Capitol* each morning and evening, hauling coal to feed the forges, washing linen for the officers' mess, and carrying water buckets to the dozen or so work parties. All this work was done in boiling heat and under a constant plague of flies, redbugs, and gnats during the day, mosquitoes at night. Half the work force suffered from either malaria or dysentery. I had the "trots" five days running after clearing the latrine. Albert had an even worse case.

Everything done at the yard was in haste and against the clock. Iron scoured from the countryside arrived daily by wagon and was pounded into armor for the *Arkansas*. Timber for the gun carriages to cradle the heavy iron cannons had to be felled and supplied to a building firm in Canton. Ordinance— gunpowder and shot—had to be rushed from warehouses as far away as Virginia.

Among the work details I enjoyed most was helping the carpenters and engineers onboard the *Arkansas*. Inside the hull it was hot and airless, and the work was tedious—sweeping up wood shavings, sanding smooth the planking. But I got to see the boat taking shape: the gun deck; the pilot house; all the various bunkers for food, water, coal, ammunition; and the boilers and steam engines with their gleaming pistons and gears.

One such day I was assigned to a carpentry detail under a civilian overseer named Adams from Coxburg up in Holmes County. He was a portly man, always breathless and beet-red in the face from the heat. Four of us worked that morning in what was to be the wardroom. Adams chewed sweet tobacco constantly and carried with him a chipped porcelain cream jug into which he spat out the juice. To me fell the task of emptying this jug when it threatened to overflow.

That morning the boat was a hive of activity. The engineering crew had finished reassembling the two engines, and there was to be a first test run. Firemen had the boilers stoked and the steam up, which raised the temperature in the hull and gun deck an extra fifteen degrees at least. Adams looked set to pass out.

"Be a lad," he said, holding out the spit jug for the third time that day. "Dump this in the river."

Climbing the ladder to the open bow hatch, I felt the ship lurch. Tobacco juice swilled out onto my shoes. I poked my head above deck and found the *Arkansas* cast off from the wharf and adrift on the Yazoo. Thick black smoke belched from the iron stack. Another lurch and a roar from the engines and she turned into the current. A cheer rose from a small crowd of workmen on the bank as the ship began to steam slowly upstream.

I dared not climb out into view. Brown himself was up above the pilothouse. I heard the shout:

"Take her full steam!"

And the *Arkansas* groaned and rattled; pistons drove cranks, turning the two screw propeller shafts. Dead into the current she plowed, making about four knots. In the slack water before the first bend she hit six, about the speed of a horse at a slow trot.

Half an hour later we turned and steamed back downriver. I had returned below, but then Brown gave all the work crews leave to come up on deck. Adams and the rest of the men stood with their cigars and pipes, enjoying the breeze. The ship slowed as the pilot maneuvered her toward the banks of the naval yard. But then she suddenly lurched to port and, to everyone's surprise, turned a full circle mid-river before easing up again beside the *Capitol*. An automatic stopper had failed on one of the engines, and the starboard propeller kept churning after the other had shut down. Engineers found the fault difficult to repair. It wasn't the last time the *Arkansas* would perform this little trick.

~

Our second Sunday at the yard, Brown worked only half the crews in split shifts, and we boys were given the afternoon off. Wallace came looking for me just after lunch. He was on guard duty at the gate.

"Two ladies to see you," he said with the same dull grin. "One of 'em got a gammy leg, but she sure looks sweet."

"Thanks. That'll be my little sister."

Wallace looked stricken. "Sorry, Sam. I meant no offense."

"That's okay. Don't worry," I said and followed him back to the gate.

"Say, do you think they might have brung some licorice?"

"I seriously doubt it, Wallace."

He sighed and returned to his post.

Martha and Liz stood by the wagon, dressed from Sunday service. Cope sat up in the driver seat and touched his hat brim when he saw me. Martha gave me a tearful hug. Liz looked disappointed.

"Where's your uniform?" she asked.

"Nice to see you, too." I kissed her cheek. "We haven't been issued uniforms yet."

Martha took both my hands.

"You look thin. And sunburnt as a farmer."

"Yeah, well. They confiscated my parasol. So how's Grandfather? Is he angry with me?"

Martha shook her head. "Just worried. We all miss you, Sam, even Liz."

"Hardly," Liz replied, and smiled over at Hector leering from the guard hut. "The pigs are getting fat without you around to clear the table. Otherwise, life goes on."

"Pay her no mind," said Martha. "Grandfather asked that you come home for a visit first leave you get."

She brushed away a tear. "Promise?"

"Of course I will."

We talked for about a quarter of an hour in the shade of the wagon. Martha then reached behind the seat and retrieved a book, along with a parcel tied with string.

"I picked this up at the library," she said and handed me the book. "Do you get much free time?"

"Some. Thank you."

"Here's another little treat." And she gave me the parcel. "Not sure it's traveled well. Share it with Albert and anyone else."

"Except the Yankees, of course," Liz added and climbed up into the wagon. "Let's go. I'm sweating."

Martha gave me another hug and I helped her up into the seat. Cope tipped his hat and drove away. I turned my head as I passed the gate so as not to give Hector the satisfaction of my tears.

Inside the parcel was a pound cake with strawberry sugar glaze.

~

A breeze picked up later in the afternoon. Albert and I found a shady spot by the river and ate half the cake. I started my new book. It was *The Pickwick Papers* by

Dickens, a welcome change from the Tennyson. Albert pulled out his calculus text and promptly fell asleep. In the distance I could hear Dermot Conroy, the twins' older brother, playing a sad tune on his Irish whistle.

Not far away a group of riverboat men including Bixby and Wilson had laid out a canvas tarp and were shooting dice with a watchful eye for officers, as Brown had forbidden gambling. Autin loitered over the game. I was too far away to hear, but it looked obvious that he was trying hard to be one of the men. Each time a player rolled a high score he'd whoop and clap and carry on. I heard someone finally snap:

"Keep it down, dumbhead."

But Autin paid no heed. Bixby then bent to throw, and when the dice landed Autin shouted, "Damn, Bix! You're on a roll."

Roll or not, the cook had had enough by then. He grabbed Autin's shirtfront and gave him a violent shove. The boy fell backward over some oak roots. All the men laughed and then resumed the game. Autin lay there grinning like he was somehow in on the joke.

Watching this gave me some satisfaction. Autin had been a jerk from day one. He never missed an opportunity to ride me or Albert about being "tenderfoots" or "schoolgirls." To hear him brag you'd think he'd captained a Mississippi steamboat rather than just worked as a cabin boy emptying chamber pots. He'd drank, he'd gambled, he'd whored, he'd fought men twice his size. It was impossible to know when he was telling the truth. Never once did he ask anything about me or Albert.

After a while Autin lost interest in the game and drifted away. No one seemed to notice or care. He strolled over to our patch of shade.

"So what's doing in the book corner?"

Albert awoke with a start and slapped at an ant crawling up his neck. Autin rolled his eyes. He then spotted the parcel with the cake and crouched down for a closer look.

"Yum. Yum. Who's this for?"

I put my book down. "Not you."

"Come on," he said. "Just a taste."

"No."

He shrugged and reached for the cake.

"Don't touch it. I'm warning you."

Albert frowned at me. "Come on, Sam. What's the big deal?"

But I'd taken enough of Autin's crap. "He's not getting one crumb."

Autin laughed. "So how you gonna stop me?"

He tore off a chunk of cake with his fingers. I leaned over and shoved him hard back into the grass. Autin sprang to his feet.

"You done it now, mister."

I stood up and took a step toward him. A look of doubt passed over his face but he stood his ground. I shoved him again and said, "Come on, Autin. What now?"

This was different from facing Butler in the bull pit. I had at least three inches on Autin and about twenty pounds. We'd caught the attention of the crap game. The men whooped and ran over to watch us.

Autin's eyes darted from them to me. My blood was up and I shoved him again. Autin raised his fists but did nothing.

Bixby walked up. "Come on now. Get to it."

Autin lurched forward and threw a halfhearted punch, so slow and predictable a granny could have dodged it. The blow glanced off my shoulder. I jabbed hard with my right fist square in his face. He fell back on his rear with his hand over a bloody nose. A roar of approval arose from the gathering crowd of men.

"Get up, Autin!" Bixby shouted. "Just a little blood. Show him how tough you are."

And that brought laughter. Autin got to his feet unsteadily, then lowered his head and ran toward me for a tackle. He hit me at the waist and pushed with his legs, trying to knock me off balance. I drove a knee into his face and heard his teeth click together hard. But he held on and I spun him about.

Bixby called, "Hell, Autin. He don't wanna dance."

Again laughter. I reached behind my back and easily wrenched his arms apart, and then I stepped aside, letting him fall into the dirt. He got up again. Blood dripped off his chin; tears streaked down his flushed cheeks.

"Are you crying?" Bixby spat.

And Autin came at me again, throwing wild punches. I ducked low and drove my right fist up hard into the side of his jaw. His knees buckled and he dropped like a sack. I then felt Albert pulling on my arm.

"Enough, Sam."

I looked up and saw Collins standing in the crowd opposite. He shook his head and pushed through the men in front of him.

Bixby was shouting. "Get up, Autin! You ain't that hurt. Gonna let that schoolboy have the last punch?"

But Autin just lay still in the dirt with his face tucked under his arm. Collins knelt down and laid a hand on his shoulder. The crowd began to scatter.

"That's right, Collins. Give him a cuddle," said Bixby. "You two deserve each other."

He walked away back to his crap game.

Albert held me by the elbow. But I yanked loose. "The guy had it coming."

He turned and picked up our books and the cake. "Maybe."

"Maybe nothing."

But I'd already begun to feel doubtful. It'd been just too easy—his bull, his bravado paper-thin. One thing about that fight, though. It did get me noticed. Later that evening I served out potatoes in the mess. A loud Irish coal heaver named Sullivan stood first in line. "Look here!" he called out. "Got the hellcat serving tatties. Good on you, son."

There was a cheer and laughter. I felt myself blush. And on down the line of hungry men, every time I heaped a plate with mash, I got winks and friendly banter. I then noticed Collins watching me as he served out hot coffee at the end of the line.

Autin worked the officers' mess that night as usual.

A large purple bruise surrounded one eye, and his nose looked thick and swollen. He did his work without any of the usual banter and then at quitting time went straight to his bunk. Collins and I and the twins were left to wash pots and clean the galley. I swept the floor and wiped the tables in the dining hall, and put out the lanterns. Bixby and the twins had by then finished up in the galley, and I went to check that everything was stowed for morning. I noticed a faint light in the storeroom and assumed someone had left a candle burning. Peering in, I found Collins sitting at the small pine table Bixby used to keep his accounts and to cheat his fellow sailors in not-so-secret poker games. It was a small, cramped room with floor-to-ceiling shelves crowded with pots and pans, sacks of flour and corn and coffee, jars of fruit, tinned goods, and other provisions.

Collins sat drinking the last dregs of coffee and having a smoke. I noticed again the shake in his hand as he reached for his pipe.

"Sorry," I said. "Didn't know you were here."

I turned to go but he called out, "Come pull up a chair. Just killing some time."

So I went in and sat at the table. "One hell of a day," I sighed, trying to make conversation.

Collins took a long draw on his pipe and blew the smoke out into the air above me. "Do you remember the yellow fever epidemic of '53?"

It was an odd question, out of nowhere.

"Yes," I replied. "We had to leave our house in town

and move up to my grandfather's farm. My father had to cancel his business trips. New Orleans got hit worst. Were you down there?"

Collins shook his head. "Far away, thank God. Sailing on a merchant ship out of Barbados, blissfully flush with rum. But I've heard the stories."

He began to tell me what he knew. How the disease was thought to have spread to New Orleans from Jamaica. How the first death had occurred in late May, an Irish laborer fresh off an emigrant ship. Within four months over ten thousand people, a tenth of the city's population, were dead. More than two hundred people died each day at the peak of the epidemic. Entire families perished within hours. Open wagons rolled through the streets with the drivers calling, "Bring out your dead." Corpses, swollen and rotting in the heat, were stacked like cordwood in the cemeteries. Gravediggers buried the dead in shallow pits, but heavy rains washed away the soil, exposing again the horror and stench.

"No worse place on earth that summer," said Collins.

I wondered why he was telling me all this. It made me sick just listening.

"Did you know Autin grew up in New Orleans?" he said. "Seven years old that summer, and he lived through it untouched, at least physically."

Collins told me how Autin was born in the Irish Channel district. His mother came from Dublin. His father was a French Creole, married into a rich New

Orleans family, with a string of mistresses of whom Autin's mother was just one. He never acknowledged Jordi as his son. The summer of 1853, Autin's mother worked as a laundress in one of the large hotels on Royal Street, and they lived together in a single room in a rundown tenement near the wharfs. One night she collapsed on the bed they shared, racked with fever and vomiting. By morning she was dead. None of the neighbors dared touch the body, so Autin had to drag her out to the street. His last look at his mother was as they trundled her away in an open wagon heaped with corpses.

Autin ended up in an orphanage kept by the Sisters of Charity, overrun with other "plague orphans." He ran away at age ten and lived on the streets until finding work on the boats, first as a cook's helper and then later as a cabin boy.

"Closest thing to family he's known since his mama died is Bixby, if you can believe that," Collins went on. "They been sailing together for the last four years."

I didn't know what to say. My hardships seemed nothing in comparison.

Collins relit his pipe. "I'm not trying to give you grief. Just thought it might explain a few things about Jordi. He's not such a bad kid, just bitter. Looks at somebody like you and sees all he's been denied in life, even if it ain't true. I think he's been long overdue a good kicking. If it wasn't you, it would've been somebody else. But one thing he don't need now is another enemy."

Collins reached into his back pocket and pulled out a tin flask.

"And I got nothing more to say on the matter. To better days," he said and took a long swig. "Now go on to bed."

Images from the fight crowded my thoughts. How could I have been so mindless, so brutal? Albert had understood. Why hadn't I? I walked slowly back to our quarters and resolved to make amends at the first opportunity. Albert and the Conroys sat on the floor playing poker. Autin lay up on his bunk reading his newspaper. I walked over and held out my hand.

"Just want to apologize. I had no cause making such a fuss over a piece of cake. It was foolish and I'm sorry it ended the way it did."

Autin lowered his newspaper and looked down at my outstretched hand. He then raised the paper again without a word.

"That's fair enough," I said. "Sorry probably ain't sufficient."

I sat down with Albert and the twins. They stared at me in disbelief.

"Go on then," I said. "Deal me in."

We played poker with goober nuts for chips. Over the last weeks Albert had developed a surprising aptitude at cards. Math did seem to matter when it came to poker. That night he won the first three hands in a row. Autin peered over his paper to watch. When Albert took the fourth with only a pair of tens, Autin groaned, "You suckers are hopeless."

He slid down off his bunk. "Deal me in before the beanpole bleeds you dry."

We all laughed, and he pushed in beside me. Simon dealt an extra hand. I brought out the cake and the five of us feasted on the remnants down to the last crumb.

7

Toward the end of June the crew of the *Arkansas* began to make preparations for the first sortie downriver. For five days we were worked beyond endurance to finish outfitting the ship. It took a full ten hours to load provisions and ordinance: foodstuff, medicine, tools, powder, shell and shot for the cannons, small arms and ammunition. Sailors pushed heavy drays back and forth across the gangplanks from the shore, over the main deck of the *Capitol,* and then out to the *Arkansas.* We worked in human chains, passing crates and sacks and barrels taken from the drays man-to-man down hatches and passageways to designated holds deep in the hull of the ship. Quartermaster Eagan directed the work, watch in hand, barking commands over a constant din of hammers and saws as civilian carpenters struggled to finish their work.

Just hours before departure, ship workers set the last segment of rail iron cladding in place over the wooden casemate. Blacksmiths had labored all night to finish fitting iron shielding to the oak-encased pilot-house. Two of the ship's ten iron cannons still lay under canvas in wooden stocks on the bank. Delivery of the last two timber gun carriages from Canton had been delayed, and Captain Brown had decided not to wait. The ship would have to return later to Yazoo City to pick them up.

That final night before departure we didn't get back to quarters until near midnight. I collapsed on my bunk and kicked off my shoes. Just then Eagan appeared in the doorway. He held five parcels wrapped in string and brown paper.

"Done good work today, boys," he said and tossed us one each. "I can't have you shipping out tomorrow not looking the part."

Inside the parcels were uniforms: two blue open-neck shirts, two pairs of blue bell-bottom trousers, a black silk neckerchief, and a black flat cap.

"Not strictly regulation," said Eagan. "Property of the U.S. Navy, in fact. But beggars can't be choosers."

He left us to try them on. Mine fit perfectly, but the sleeves of Albert's shirt rode almost halfway up his forearms and the trousers left his ankles bare.

"Least you'll stay dry longest if we sink," said Autin. We all laughed.

He had a piece of broken mirror that he used for shaving—more pretend than necessary—and stood admiring himself, adjusting the angle of his cap.

"Can't wait 'til we liberate New Orleans. Think I'll do just fine in these duds."

"You're worse than my sister at her vanity table," I said.

He ignored the comment and tucked a brown curl into place. "No point denying the truth."

A fight then broke out among the twins over caps. Simon accused Peter of stealing his and it came to blows. Albert and I wrenched them apart.

Autin held up both disputed caps. "Come on now, boys. Not one stitch different."

Later, fully uniformed and standing opposite each other, the Conroy twins appeared like one sailor in a looking glass.

Next day the CSS *Arkansas* cast off ropes and swung into the slow current of the Yazoo on active duty. It was the twenty-sixth of June and my sixteenth birthday. We'd been standing at our stations inside the gun deck for nearly an hour before the boat departed. A mid-afternoon sun beat down on the ironclad casemate, making the interior hot as a bread oven. Sweat trickled from my every pore, soaking into my shirt and trousers. A couple of men had already fainted and been pulled out onto the forward deck. The crew cheered when the engines finally roared to life and the ship lurched into motion, bringing a welcome breeze through the open gun ports.

I'd been waiting for this moment for weeks, months, maybe all my life. I was going to war. No game, no boyhood fantasy. This was real. I grinned across the deck at Albert, who stood among his gun crew next to the massive black iron barrel of a

Dahlgren naval cannon. He gave me a nervous smile. My crew manned the two forward cannons opposite, under the command of Lieutenant Gift.

No one told us our destination that day, but word round the crew was Liverpool Landing, about twenty-five miles downriver. Here Confederate troops had constructed a log barricade across the river to discourage Yankee gunboats steaming up to Yazoo City. Below the barrier three Confederate gunboats—the *Livingstone,* the *General Polk,* and the *Van Dorn*— guarded the river under the command of a jittery "Old Navy" officer named Pinkney. His orders were to keep the three ships ready for action: moored with their bows downstream, steam pressure up in the boilers, engines primed and ready to ram any Federal vessel that ventured upriver.

Just after the *Arkansas* got underway that day, Lieutenant Gift gathered together the gun crews for a brief "welcome." He wore his full uniform, and his long fair hair was matted with sweat. The men crowded into the front half of the gun deck to listen. It was a mixed group of veteran sailors, riverboat men, soldiers requisitioned from a Missouri artillery regiment, and tenderfoots like me.

Gift patted the muzzle of the massive forward Columbiad cannon. "Anyone care to tell me what this is?" he shouted.

A snort of laughter arose from some of the Missouri boys. A long, lanky soldier named Appleton piped: "Church bell?"

More laughter. Tanner pushed in among the crowd. He was Gift's gun captain on the forward Dahlgren, a small, thick-necked man with a bushy red mustache. "Stow that crap, mister," he spat up into Appleton's face. "And you address an officer as sir."

"Yes sir. Sorry, sir," Appleton replied without much conviction.

Gift smiled. "Well, I'll tell you what it ain't—some pea-shooting, mule-drawn artillery piece from your grandpap's day, such as you Missouri boys'll be used to. This is a modern naval gun. So forget all you think you know about gunnery. And if you feel the urge at any time to offer up a helpful hint or suggestion, don't. There's only one way to operate these guns, and that's my way. Listen, do as ordered, and we got no problems. Show any insubordination, and I'll have you flogged—another fine naval tradition."

Gift then had Tanner run through the gunnery drill. I never knew so much was involved with sponges and cartridge sacks, primer tubes and lanyards. Tanner led us out onto the bow deck to show us the heavy iron shutters lowered over the gun ports to protect the crew during loading. I felt fresh streams of sweat trickling down my back under the afternoon sun. But at least there was a breeze.

The sound of galloping hooves drew our attention. Two mounted soldiers in gray rode along the bank toward us and pulled up reins. Captain Brown had made his office under a canvas awning on the upper deck.

One of the riders called out, "Message from Commander Pinkney."

Brown stood up from his writing table and put on his cap. "Go ahead, soldier."

"Commander's compliments, sir. We got word of two enemy steamers just a mile downstream of our lower river batteries."

Just as he spoke we heard the distant rumble of cannon fire.

"Sounds like they've introduced themselves," said Brown. "Does Commander Pinkney have his ships at battle stations?"

The messenger, a burly, black-eyed cavalryman with a heavy beard, struggled to keep his horse under control with the rattle of our engines. He removed his hat and looked sheepish.

"No sir. Engines cold."

Brown shook his head in disbelief. I heard Tanner mutter, "Damnation."

A map was spread out on the table. The captain leaned over it, putting on his bifocals. "How much further to Liverpool Landing?"

"'Bout six miles," said the messenger.

Brown looked at his watch. "Three-thirty. Ride on back and tell Commander Pinkney we'll be there in under an hour."

One of the veteran sailors stood next to me. "What's going on?" I asked him.

"Old Pinkney, the fool, let his boilers go cold on the *Van Dorn* and them other two ships," said the man.

"Takes hours to get steam back up. So they'll just be sitting there like tin targets at a fun fair."

Tanner ordered us back through the open port into the gun deck. Just then Lieutenant Stevens came down from the upper deck. He was executive officer on the *Arkansas*, Brown's second in command, a thin, grave-looking man, though not much older than Gift and Read.

"Mr. Gift," he said. "Man the port-bow gun and fire two charges to let Commander Pinkney know we're coming."

Tanner began to holler out the names of regular experienced sailors who then ran forward and took up positions by the big forward Columbiad. A gun that size required a crew of at least fourteen men.

"Load and fire, Mr. Tanner," said Lieutenant Gift when the gun crew was assembled. With everyone working flat-out over the last few weeks to get the *Arkansas* battle ready, there had been little time for gunnery training. Gift turned to the rest of the men.

"Watch how it's done. Looks like we might not have time for patient instruction."

Both bow Columbiads sat mounted on iron rail tracks. Two side-tackle men unlashed the port gun and rolled it back into loading position. Tanner shouted a series of commands as the crew prepared and loaded the cannon.

"Serve vent and sponge. Charge with cartridge and wad only. Run out."

A man called the "loader" pushed in a powder cartridge and then a cloth wad, shoving each down the barrel with a wooden ramrod. No shot, as Brown only wanted to make noise.

At Tanner's command of "Run out," the two side-tackle men hauled away at the heave ropes to pull the gun barrel forward through the open port. Tanner shouted "Prime!" and another man stuck a wire-like tool down the gun vent to prick the cartridge. He then inserted a primer tube that would generate spark to ignite the charge when the gun captain pulled an attached lanyard cord. He held up a clenched fist and shouted, "Ready!" The crew stepped away from the gun.

Tanner looked to Lieutenant Gift, who nodded. Tanner then yelled, "Fire!" and pulled the lanyard.

I wasn't ready for the force of that blast at such close quarters. The concussion wave hit my face like a slap and tore at my eardrums. The gun screeched back along the iron rails, hitting wooden chocks to stop its recoil.

A buzzing filled my ears such that I could scarcely hear. Lieutenant Stevens shouted more orders, and the gun deck erupted in chaos. Men pushed in all directions, and gun captains hollered at their crews, directing frantic drills for men who had never yet fired a naval gun in practice, much less battle. No one expected the prospect of a fight in the first three hours of duty.

Tanner prepared the forward cannon for a second

signal charge. I picked a moment when he didn't seem occupied and touched his elbow. He turned to me in distracted fury. "What do you want, boy?"

"S-sorry, sir," I stammered. "What am I supposed to do now?"

"Do? Go to hell for a start," he shouted. Then he turned away and hurled a string of abuse at a crewman who had managed to tangle a heave rope.

Someone grabbed my collar. It was Wikers, one of the friendlier midshipmen. He spoke close to my ear.

"Go see Master Milliken down in the forward magazine. He'll get you sorted."

"Thank you. Sir."

I turned away and collided with another sailor. He had a sack of sand and was spreading it across the planking of the deck by the handful. For what reason I knew not.

"Sorry," I muttered.

"Ee-jit," he grunted in reply, an Irishman.

I shoved my way around the pilothouse platform and reached the forward hatch. I climbed down the ladder to the orlop deck and made my way along the dimly lit passage toward the forward magazine. In the shell room a sailor stood loading iron shot onto wooden racks. I asked for the master gunner and he pointed further forward.

The thick oaken hatch to the powder magazine had been latched open. Across the inside opening hung a white canvas sheet. A dim light glowed through the cloth, and I could hear voices inside. I reached out and pushed aside the canvas. It was damp to the touch. Milliken and another man stood with their backs to the door. Both wore what looked like white artist smocks and canvas slip-on shoes. Milliken held a magazine lantern over racks of powder kegs, calling out numbers to the other man, who wrote them in a jotter. A third man sat on a crate, measuring out gunpowder from an opened keg into woolen cartridge bags.

I stepped through the hatch. The wet sheet dropped behind me.

"Pardon, sir," I said.

Both men swung about in sudden alarm. Milliken's face turned red with fury. "Out, you damned fool!"

He rushed over and in one motion swept aside the sheet and shoved me hard back through the hatch. I thumped my head on the low lintel.

"Don't ever come in here, boy. Kick a spark off a nail on them boots and blow us all to kingdom come."

"Sorry, sir. I was told to report—"

But he cut me short. "Not here." And he pushed back through the canvas.

I now had no idea where to go or what to do, so I made my way up the passage past the shell room, back to the forward ladder. Here I wedged myself against one of the oaken ribs and the hull, out of harm's way, and sat there feeling useless, wondering what the other boys were up to.

In the dim light something warm and wet brushed against my fingers. I jumped in alarm and banged my head again. It was Lieutenant Barbot's dog, Nick. Barbot was one of the senior officers, a Creole from New Orleans, and Nick was unofficial ship's mascot, a Jack Russell terrier no bigger than a large rat. Nick had been sailing with Barbot since he was smuggled aboard a U.S. naval frigate as a pup. But now he was a fervent Reb with the run of the boat. He was also possibly the smartest dog in the Confederacy. Barbot had only to ask for a particular item in his cabin—pipe, Bible, brush—and Nick would fetch it without error. Some evenings Barbot brought out his guitar and played minstrel tunes for the crew. Nick would dance in circles on his hind legs and perform twisting leaps for scraps of beef or chicken. Barbot told us that after the war he planned to take Nick across the ocean and make his fortune touring the royal courts of Europe.

Nick jumped in my lap and rolled onto his back for a tummy rub. Sailors clambered up and down the ladder, all in a rush. Nobody seemed to notice us tucked away in that corner.

After a while, Quartermaster Eagan passed on his way to the forward magazine. "What in hell are you doing hiding there in the dark?" he hollered. Nick growled at the interruption and then scampered away.

"Waiting for orders, sir."

"Orders? Here's one then, you sorry son of a bitch. Go report to Cook and do something useful."

So that's how I ended up peeling potatoes in the galley with Bixby as the *Arkansas* steamed toward her first engagement. Bixby stood chopping meat in his bloody apron with both a cutlass and a pistol tucked into his belt, protection against boarders. He found it highly amusing having me for mess duty with the ship at battle stations.

"Tell you what, Wood," he said. "Some Yankee tries to raid our kitchen, I shoot 'em, you peel 'em." He laughed and tossed more beef into his stew pot.

To be stuck below was nerve wracking, waiting blind for the fighting to start, no chance for even a glimpse of the enemy. Each blow of Bixby's cleaver made me think the bombardment had begun, and he chuckled to watch me jump.

My misery soon came to an end when Midshipman Scales appeared at the hatch with his usual look of bland contempt. "Captain wants water," he said, and nothing more.

Bixby cursed him under his breath and ordered me to get to it. I filled a tin pitcher from the water barrel and placed it on a tray with four cups. It was a relief to get out into the fresh air again. Captain Brown and Lieutenant Stevens stood under the awning on the upper spar deck along with Scales and Midshipman Wikers. I placed the tray on a table and began to pour out water into the cups. I took my time, not wanting to go back below and miss the action.

Brown and the officers stared intently downstream as the *Arkansas* rounded a bend of cypress. Three gunboats, converted side-wheel steamers, came slowly into view, moored along one bank behind a large floating barricade of timber and other wooden debris stretching the full width of the river. These were the Confederate gunboats under Pinkney's command, charged with guarding the upper Yazoo river valley. Black smoke and flame billowed from the gun ports of the nearest boat, and wisps drifted out the ventilation grating of the second. Not a single Yankee gunboat was in sight.

"Damned coward," Lieutenant Stevens muttered.

"Enough of that," said Brown. "Get some fire crews into the boats. See what we can salvage."

Stevens slid down the angled front deck of the casemate and hollered into the gun ports. "Fire crews, topside, double time."

Brown croaked, "Where's that drink?"

I held out a cup. "Here, sir. Begging your pardon. But what's happening?"

Scales gave me a sharp look, but Brown seemed unbothered by my question. "Commander Pinkney obviously values discretion over valor and has chosen to burn his ships, enemy unseen. We beg to differ."

Sailors lowered both of the *Arkansas* launch boats and held them alongside as fire divisions boarded with axes and buckets. The men set their oars and rowed toward the bank to portage the barricade. Hauling both of the launch boats up the bank and relaunching them downstream of the barricade allowed just enough time for the fires to take hold aboard both wooden gunboats. Howling drafts up the stacks of the *Livingstone* turned her decks into a red raging inferno.

Our boats could not get near. Soon her mooring ropes snapped, and she drifted down and snagged against the smoldering *General Polk*.

The *General Polk* was quickly engulfed, and her mooring ropes gave way, too. Both blazing wrecks drifted lazily downstream toward the veteran gunboat *Van Dorn*, which for some reason had been spared Pinkney's torches. Our men had managed to axe the mooring ropes and attach towlines to the *Van Dorn*, but her hull lay grounded in the soft mud and she couldn't be budged.

The entire crew of the *Arkansas*, over two hundred men, crowded onto the outer decks to watch the catastrophe. The burning wrecks smashed against the *Van Dorn* with a splintering crack, and the flames took fully hold, leaping into the sky over the river. Sparks set light to nearby trees and the fire spread into the woods along the bank.

Stevens trained his telescope downriver and caught sight of a Federal ram watching smugly beyond range of our downstream gun batteries. "Three Confederate gunboats destroyed with barely a shot fired," he said bitterly. Now only the river barricade and a few cannon emplacements along the bluffs stood between the Federals and the upper Yazoo river valley—and of course the *Arkansas*.

～

The *Arkansas* remained moored at Liverpool Landing for the next five days, but the Federals kept away downriver. Apart from the usual routine of mess duty and washing down the decks, our days were spent in endless drills. Quartermaster Eagan took charge of training us boys and the rest of the new recruits. We learned how to load and fire a long-barreled musket and how to fix a bayonet on the end of the barrel and charge screaming at burlap sacks of hay—or, in Albert's case, how to trip and jam your finger over the trigger, blowing a hole in the ground a few inches from Eagan's boot. I soon knew how to gut a man with a cutlass or cut his throat, at least in theory.

Master Gunner Milliken instructed me, Albert, and the twins in our main duty during battle: running powder and shot to the gun crews. Powder charges were delivered in color-coded cartridge bags carried in a leather-covered "pass box." Our task seemed to me ridiculously simpleminded, and I guessed this was why we were called "powder monkeys."

The first night on the boat we slept among the guns inside the casemate, but it grew so airless and smelly that the next night most men spread bedrolls along the bank. One of the Missourians rolled onto a cotton-mouth moccasin, and the snake bit him on the ass. Our surgeon Mr. Case made one of his orderlies suck out the venom and the poor man never lived it down. But the Missourian survived.

That same night, just a few hours before sunrise, a distant roar aroused the crew. Flashes lit the western horizon in an unending sequence that glowed on the faces of the watching men. Word had come the day before that Farragut had moved his entire fleet just below Vicksburg.

"By God," said Collins. "Somebody's taking a pounding."

I shivered, even though the night was warm.

Next afternoon Bixby had me washing the officers' linen in a tub by the river. Lieutenant Read appeared out of the gun deck of the *Arkansas* and bounced down the gangplank whistling "The Bonny Blue Flag." He passed me and touched two fingers to his brow in a jaunty salute. A few steps on he stopped in his tracks and turned back.

"Hey, Wood. You up for a little pleasure cruise?"

"Sir?" I replied.

"Come on. Follow me."

"But what about Mr. Bixby's—" I began.

"Bixby's laundry can wait."

So I rolled down my sleeves and retrieved my cap. I followed Read down to the wharf where a small steam tug lay moored. Her boiler was stoked, and her stack reeked a thin, black smoke. Read leapt aboard her bow. He then beckoned to me.

"Hop on. We ain't got all day."

I jumped aboard just as the mate cast off lines. Read waved to the tug captain in his pilot house and we steamed away downstream. I looked back at the receding wharf.

"Beg pardon, sir," I asked, trying not to let my nerves betray me. "Where are we going?"

Just two days earlier a Federal gunboat had been

on the prowl not far downstream. Read grinned. "Going to fight the fleet. I got my pistol." He patted the holster on his belt. "What you got?"

"Nothing, sir."

"Then you'll just have to spit at 'em."

Read laughed without concern and took off his hat to let the breeze catch his long, brown hair. I felt an urge to jump overboard.

"Don't worry," he said. "Captain just wants me to take a few soundings, test the river depth over the sandbar down at Satartia. Thought you might enjoy the ride."

"Thank you, sir," I said, trying to sound enthusiastic.

The captain of the tug was a fellow named Finlayson, a sun-cured old man missing an eye to cancer. His boat had been requisitioned for service in the Confederate Navy. As protection from enemy fire he'd roped a few bales of cotton to his bow and pilothouse.

"A cotton-clad," Read joked. He leaned back against one of the bales and fired up a cigar. I think the only reason he ordered me along was for some company. He did most all the talking, his favorite topic being Charles W. Read. I got pretty much his entire life history, and to be fair it made a good tale in parts.

Read told me that he left home at sixteen to attend the Naval Academy. Before that he worked as a printer's apprentice. A rich planter uncle from over the river in Arkansas agreed to sponsor him at Annapolis. He graduated last in the class of 1860. It seemed almost a point of pride to him.

"Hell, if you can't be first," he said, "then best be last. Least that marks you out as exceptional."

When Mississippi voted to secede from the Union, Read was serving as a midshipman onboard the USS *Powhatan* off the coast of Vera Cruz. He tendered his resignation immediately.

"Nearly joined the Confederate infantry in a moment of patriotic fervor," he said. "Thankfully sense prevailed—just a damn turkey shoot, that."

Read enlisted in the Confederate Navy and served on an eight-gun steamer called the *McRae*, which fought battles up and down the Mississippi in the first year of the war. The *McRae* was part of the ragtag Confederate fleet assembled to defend the river below New Orleans. Lieutenant Read was serving second in command the night Admiral Farragut sailed the Union fleet, ship after ship, past the blazing guns of Fort Jackson and Fort St. Philip. It was a passage said to be "impassable."

"Night bright as day with fire rafts and burning ships, flares streaking out over the river," said Read, puffing on his cigar that sunny afternoon. "We were right in the thick of the fight, along with the *Manassas*. No problem finding something to fire at, sloops and gunboats on every side of us. Soon the *McRae* was riddled with shot. Then an enemy shell pierced our deck and exploded in the sail room next to the magazine. A fire broke out, and I had to go below to help put it out before the powder ignited and blew us into tomorrow. Few minutes later this big gunboat fired a massive broadside across our deck—grape and canister. Tore away the wheel ropes and most of the rigging. Killed Captain Huger."

Read shook his head. "Ship that done it had No. 6 on its funnel. Next time I see the bastard, he's sunk."

The lieutenant then rose to his feet and peered downstream.

"Nearly crapped my britches that night," he said. "Any man tells you he's not afraid in a hot fight is either a liar or crazy. But by God, Wood, there's nothing like it! Working those guns as though each second may be your last. Never felt more alive. You'll understand, when the time comes."

But I wondered how I would react in battle. I'd heard of armies retreating in blind panic. Officers shooting soldiers in the back as they ran from the enemy. But where could you run to on a boat? Maybe not being able to run would be a good thing.

~

Soon we reached the bar at Satartia. Read asked the captain to ferry the full breadth of the Yazoo as he used sounding ropes to measure the river depth. He called out readings and I recorded them in a notebook.

"Eight, ten, sixteen—"

Just then Finlayson called out, "We got a visitor astern."

A quarter mile downstream a Federal gunboat appeared around a bend in the river. It was a side-wheel steamer with a gun mounted on its bow. Read shouted at Finlayson to keep her steady, that he had a few more soundings to take. Just then we heard a thundering boom. A ring of smoke puffed out across the water from the boat's bow. I ducked behind one of the cotton bales, as if that would make any difference. The shot landed with a large splash about thirty yards short of us.

Read looked up in surprise. "I'll be damned. Bastard's ranging for us. Not much of a shot."

Finlayson's one good eye opened wide as a silver dollar.

"Guess we better skedaddle," Read called out.

Finlayson soon had the tug running flat out upriver. I sat up just behind the bow, silently urging it to go faster. But the gunboat didn't fire a second shot and made no effort to chase. My heart beat wildly for the next twenty minutes as I kept a close eye on the empty water behind us. I fancied this had been my baptism of fire. Enemy cannon, death no more than a stone's throw away. A thrill ran up my spine. I had tasted "real" battle and held firm.

8

Five days after steaming down to Liverpool Landing, the *Arkansas* returned to the shipyard at Yazoo City for last repairs and to load her two remaining guns. On the Fourth of July the captain gave us a twenty-four-hour liberty. The town had the usual festivities planned: a picnic and fireworks display. I found it odd to imagine all those celebrations happening in towns North and South, all of us hailing the same heroes, enjoying the same games, laughing at the same jokes, giving thanks over our plates to the same God. It seemed crazy to think we could be slaughtering each other by the thousands, but that was the way of it. "Theirs not to reason why / Theirs but to do and die..."

How could it be my place to question? So I just put those thoughts—and Tennyson—out of mind.

I hurried back to quarters just after the noon mess. There hadn't been enough advance notice of the shore leave to send a note up to Sandhill. But I felt certain that Cope would drive Martha and Liz down for the afternoon and I could get a night home in my own bed. Albert and the twins were dressed in fresh uniforms, but Autin lay unchanged on his bunk, reading his newspaper.

"Thought you were heading into town with Bixby and company," I said as I pulled off my damp shirt.

"Changed my mind," Autin replied, without looking away from his paper.

"Why?"

"None of your damn business."

I suspected it was Bixby's mind that had changed. No doubt they'd be heading straight to Clooney's Tavern and didn't want any kid along to spoil the party.

"Well, you can't just sit in here all day. Come with us," I urged him.

"No, thank you," he said.

"Come on. It's a fine day. May never live to see another."

"I said no."

I reached up and snatched away his newspaper. He tried to retrieve it but was too slow.

"Give it back."

"Sorry. No can do."

But Autin just lay back on his bunk. "Fine. Keep it. I don't care."

"Tell you what," I said. "We'll toss for it." I pulled out a penny. "Heads, I give back your precious newspaper. Tails, you get cleaned up and come with us."

I lost the toss, of course, but Autin decided to come

along anyway. We waited as he put on a clean uniform, and then headed out for the gate.

Hector had drawn sentry duty that day and sourly checked each of our passes before letting us go. "Try not to soil them monkey suits," he taunted as the five of us headed toward town.

Fourth of July was celebrated at the park alongside the river. That year was much like previous ones, being early in the war before the shortages. Long tables groaned with heaps of sliced ham, roast beef, fried chicken, potato salad, buttered corncobs, mash and gravy, corn bread, and all manner of cakes and pies and fresh watermelon. Two slaves from Magnolia Plantation cooked a whole hog on a spit over a large fire pit. Later in the afternoon games and contests were held. The main event was the sweepstakes, a dozen or so of the finest thoroughbred horses in the county running a five-mile circuit with a winner's purse of fifty dollars and a fortune cast in wagers.

Buggies and wagons crowded the streets. I spotted my old nemesis Wade Walton and three of his gang from the Academy lounging under the shade of an oak tree near the start line of the horserace. No Butler, though. I heard he'd run off to join the 8th Mississippi Infantry. They all went quiet and stared as we passed.

"Friends of yours?" Autin asked.

"No. Just ignore them," I said.

Walton whispered something and he and his pals laughed.

"Be damned if I will," said Autin. He walked over

and stood in front of them, holding up both his arms, turning a full circle. "Got a good look now? Want to draw a picture?"

Autin eyed Walton a good five seconds, then spat and turned away. Albert shot me a look of alarm but I just grinned.

"Must be queer on sailors," Autin said loudly as he passed.

~

Albert left us to go see his parents and the twins went with the two older Conroy brothers to visit with a cousin over from Benton. So Autin and I had a wander around. The Christian Women's Auxiliary had set up a bake sale on foldaway tables under a canvas awning next to the church. The sign read: "Penny a cake! Help buy uniforms and bandages for our brave soldiers."

Nancy Thurman sat at a table next to one of her sisters. She wore a gray dress, and her long golden hair fell down across one shoulder. When she spotted me, she waved. Frasier Melton stood by the table and followed her glance with unmasked hostility. He was two years older than me. I'd heard he was reading the law in his father's office.

I walked over to say hello but immediately became tongue-tied. So I pulled out a penny.

"May I buy a cake?"

"Sorry, Wood," Melton butted in. "Too late. They're all sold out. Best cakes in the sale."

Nancy gave a modest shrug and said, "You can buy one from Bernice."

Bernice was Nancy's older sister, though a good six inches shorter and quite a bit rounder. No more than half her lemon fairy cakes had been sold.

"Thanks. Can I buy one?" I asked her.

She looked up at me with a sour expression. "Hand over the penny."

Melton grinned. I felt tempted to ask why he'd yet to enlist like most of the men in town his age. I took the cake and thanked Bernice.

Nancy smiled. "When your boat sailed last week I thought I'd missed my chance to wish you luck."

I felt myself blush.

"So how are you finding the Naval Service?" she asked.

I had never much thought of all that pot scrubbing and ditch digging and linen washing as the Naval Service. "Not too bad," I answered. "Been hard work getting the ship battle ready. Lots of gun drills and the like. It gets tough on the ears, all the cannon fire."

Melton shifted uncomfortably. Autin snorted in amusement as he examined the remainder of Bernice's fairy cakes.

"Sorry. This here is my shipmate, Jordi Autin," I said grudgingly.

Jordi removed his cap with a flourish and tucked it under his arm. "Of the New Orleans Autins. Most pleased to make your acquaintance, Miss...?"

"Thurman," said Nancy.

"Forgive me. I do know the name. Sam has spoken highly of you. Must be my brain addled with all that cannon fire."

Nancy smiled dubiously. I gave Jordi a sharp kick in the ankle.

"I like your uniforms," she said.

Jordi put a penny on the table and winked at Bernice as he chose a fairy cake.

"Well, you should see our naval whites, Miss Thurman. Dazzling, but we reserve those only for balls and such like."

"Balls?"

"Oh yes. There's certain to be a grand ball when we sail in to liberate New Orleans."

"So you're confident of defeating the Union fleet?"

"Supremely, Miss Thurman. We'll soon send them Yanks to the muddy bottom. No fear. Did you know Admiral Farragut can't swim? Drop him in, sinks like a stone. Imagine an admiral unable to swim. Well, he'll soon regret the day he decided to set sail up the Mississippi."

I grabbed Jordi by the elbow and pulled him away from the table.

"Maybe we can talk later," I said to Nancy.

She smiled in reply.

"Yes. Until later, Miss Thurman," Jordi called.

I squeezed his arm hard.

"Ouch," he whined. "Let go. That hurts."

Out of earshot he grinned and said, "Sorry. Did I crowd your style? My, but she is a peach."

Just then I heard someone shout my name. I turned to find Martha and Liz pulling up in the buggy with Cope at the reins. Martha waved and jumped out to help Liz down the step. I ran over to meet them. Both gave me a hug and kiss, Martha bubbling as usual. Jordi stood back, studying his shoes with grim intent.

"How long do you have?" Martha asked.

"Until tomorrow afternoon."

"Good," she sniffed. "You can come home with us tonight. Grandfather will be so pleased."

Liz looked me up and down. "I thought it was the Confederate Navy you were joining. Don't the Yankees wear blue?"

Jordi stifled a laugh. Liz gave him a critical eye.

"Sorry to offend your fashion sense," I said, "but I'm sure we'll all figure out who to shoot at."

Martha smiled at Jordi. "So do we get to meet your friend?"

I made introductions. Jordi for once seemed at a loss for words, as did Liz, surprisingly.

Martha took my arm and asked Jordi polite questions as we strolled among the tables greeting people. I think she was glad for the distraction. So much bad feeling existed then for Grandfather. It was hard to predict how folks might treat us—smiles or snubs or open hostility. But Martha refused to hide away from it, and Liz always gave back as good as she got. Nevertheless, I did feel better for wearing the new uniform.

Later in the afternoon we went to watch the games.

Jordi and I entered the three-legged race and came in third. Some of the Missouri artillerymen organized a tug of war against the regular sailors. Jordi and I joined in with the sailors and collapsed in a heap when the landsmen gave up and let go the rope. Nancy Thurman stood under a parasol and laughed along with her sisters.

Jordi entered the egg race with Martha while I sat with Liz. I glanced over again at Nancy, who avoided my gaze, smiling to herself. I did manage to catch Mrs. Thurman's eye instead. She gave me a look that would sour milk.

Liz took my arm and sighed as we watched Jordi racing alongside Martha, laughing as they tried to bump the eggs off each other's spoons.

"Did Jordi really live in an orphanage?"

"So he says," I replied.

She pondered that a moment. "I never think of us as orphans. I mean, we have Grandfather and Aunt Margaret and Uncle Steven and the Morgan cousins down in Baton Rouge. Must be horrid not to have anybody."

She laid her cheek against my shoulder.

Jordi won the race and had to stand red-faced on the podium as Sarah Bryant pinned a blue ribbon to his uniform. Liz clapped loudly, shouting, "Hurrah, hurrah!"

Jordi and I put a dollar each on Arabia, the Felker's roan thoroughbred, to win the horse race. Martha pretended not to notice, being the former minister's granddaughter, but then forgot herself and shouted loudly, "Ride, ride!" as Arabia rounded the bend and thundered ahead of the field. We won five dollars in total and treated Liz and Martha to coffee and cake at the Oxford Hotel.

Just at sunset the Magnolia boys served the roasted pork. As I went to get a second helping, one of the Thurman's young Negro slaves pressed a note into my hand. It read: "Meet me in five minutes at the rope swing."

So I made an excuse to Jordi and my sisters and went to wait down by the river, heart beating at my throat. Nancy came hurrying along the path, her face flushed.

"Sorry. Hope you don't think me bold. I just didn't see how else we might talk," she said all in a rush. "My mother would never approve. She's gone home to change for the evening. Bernice is on her third plate of pork. Hard to believe sometimes we're sisters. I mean, I just eat like a bird.... Shall we walk?"

Nancy slipped her arm into mine and pulled me along the path without waiting for an answer. It was a warm evening and not much cooler in the shade of the woods along the riverbank. I felt the sweat prickling under my shirt, less from heat than from nerves. But conversation was not a problem, as Nancy did all the talking.

"Your friend Mr. Autin seems quite the gentleman. Do you think he knows Celeste Aubry? She's my second cousin down in New Orleans. The family's got a great big house on First and Prytania. Maybe he was at Gallier Hall when she made her debut."

"Maybe," I replied, somehow doubting that cabin boys frequented such affairs. "I'll certainly ask."

"I'm so glad you all turned up when you did. Frasier Melton can be such a bore. He thinks he's brilliant 'cause he's studying the law. Always trying to catch me out. 'Now, Miss Nancy, you forgot what you said at first.' Then he repeats it word for word, no matter how long or stupid. What's the use of proving I'm inconsistent? I know I am. It's just proving a fact. Facts are boring anyhow. So I just say, 'Oh, be merciful and spare me. I agree to every and all things, only spare me!'"

And she laughed and I laughed.

"I think Frasier's in love with Bernice," Nancy went on. "That's the only reason he hangs around so much. It's plain to see."

This struck me as incredible. What was plain to all, even Bernice, was that Frasier Melton had his eye firmly on Nancy. How could she be that naïve?

"Really. Do you think so?" I asked.

"Oh yes. Silly man. Bernice has already promised herself to Tom Gibson. Now him.... But I mustn't call names! It's terrible to say, but I couldn't help laughing a little to hear he'd been wounded at Shiloh. What's the use of wasting a nice big cannon ball on little Tommy Gibson, when a pea from a popgun could have done the trick? Not to say he isn't brave, like all our boys. He writes Bernice twice a week. Tells her that he thinks of her each and every minute of the day, that's it's the only thing that makes war bearable. He does write a good letter...."

She then squeezed my arm and turned away shyly.

"You can think of me, if you like. When you sail into battle. Father says any man would be fool to set foot on the *Arkansas*. How can one boat fight an entire fleet? I think he's just glad to be so old that nobody'll ask him to fight. So will you? Think of me, I mean?"

"I will," I said. Nothing grander than that came to mind.

That moment she turned and stretched up to kiss me. Her lips were so soft and full, moist from the heat of the afternoon. I was sure I'd feel that kiss forever.

Then she pushed out of my arms and hurried away up the path. I ran to catch her.

"I can't believe I just did that," she said breathlessly. "What would my mother think? I don't care! We may never get another chance. Darn this war!"

I reached again for her hand and we kissed once more. It seemed so unreal, the whole scene, like we were characters in one of Liz's English novels. We then walked another quarter mile or so until Nancy said she had to get back to her family. I was instructed to double back on the river road so that no one would see us together. I kissed her again and then took to the woods on Love's wings.

Back at the picnic Jordi sat happily between Martha and Liz, waiting for the fireworks as the sun set below the broad delta horizon. Cope stood by, chewing on a stalk of sugarcane.

"What are you grinning about?" Liz asked me.

"Nothing," I replied.

Jordi nudged her and smiled. "Might it be that Miss Thurman?"

I dropped onto the picnic blanket opposite them. "Might be."

Martha gave me a queer look and quickly changed the subject.

Each Fourth Norman Harper always took charge of the fireworks: big skyrockets ordered special from Memphis. Just as the show started I saw Collins wander up to watch. He looked pretty much three sheets to the wind already. He nodded once in our direction but no more. Every time a rocket exploded, he flinched involuntarily and took another sip from his hip flask. Liz clutched Jordi's arm and screamed in delight with each sky burst.

When the display finished we got up and folded the blankets. Cope went to get the buggy.

Jordi brushed off his uniform. "Guess I'd better head on back to the boat."

Liz moaned. "No! Not yet. We don't have to go home right away."

Martha touched my elbow. "Jordi could spend the evening with us at Sandhill."

Liz took his hand and pleaded: "Yes. Do."

"No, no. But thanks. I couldn't impose." He looked to me.

I shrugged. "Got a spare room, soft bed. I'm sure Cope would drive us both back tomorrow afternoon."

Liz grabbed Jordi's arm and pulled him toward the waiting buggy. "Sorry. No excuses." He laughed as she tugged him along.

A bright half moon rose into the sky and cast the road in a silver light. We sang as the buggy headed up into the hills: "Lorena" and "Oh! Susanna" and "A Red, Red Rose." Martha refused to sing "Dixie" as it made her think of Henry, so we sang "Yankee Doodle" instead. And I thought constantly of Nancy, that kiss still on my lips.

Grandfather and Bessie sat waiting for us out on the porch. He jumped up and met me on the steps with a firm hug. He seemed thinner in my arms, more insubstantial somehow.

"It's good to have you home, Sam."

I told him I was sorry for all the trouble I'd caused.

But he just whispered, "No apologies. Not to me."

~

Nothing more was said on the topic of war, right or wrong, as we moved in to the front parlor. Jordi and I were bombarded with questions to do with life on the *Arkansas*, her men, her officers. Grandfather opened a bottle of claret. Liz played the piano, my favorite Mozart sonata. Martha then led us in endless parlor games that continued long after Grandfather went to bed. Jordi displayed a comic talent at charades that left

Liz barely able to speak. The two of them defeated Martha and me in nearly every encounter.

Half past midnight I showed Jordi to the spare room. He stripped down to his underclothes and dropped onto the bed.

"Don't think I've ever enjoyed myself more in a day," he said, and I could tell he meant it. "Liz is great."

"Great pain in the neck."

Jordi sighed and closed his eyes. "Martha, too. You just don't know your luck."

I blew out his candle and stood a moment in the darkness. "Guess you're right. Never much thought of it."

But he was already snoring into his pillow.

~

Next morning we slept in, and Bessie cooked us a full fry-up: eggs, ham, sausages, hominy grits, buttermilk biscuits, and real coffee. Each time Jordi cleared his plate Bessie would appear again with her iron skillet.

"No, thank you," he said as she offered one last sausage. "I'm fit to burst."

"Go on." She dropped it on his plate anyway. "Nice to have boys back at my table. Nobody eats proper around here no more."

Liz sat at the table opposite, waiting for us to finish. She intended to give Jordi a tour of the farm.

"Aren't you hungry?" Jordi asked her.

"I had my breakfast *hours* ago," she replied. "A cup of tea with jam and bread."

"See what I mean?" said Bessie.

Liz ignored her. "Then I fed the chickens and wrote a letter to my cousin Ellen. Not all of us can afford to lie in bed half the day. Are you finished yet?"

"Done for," said Jordi.

He rose from the table. Liz reached for her walking stick. She rarely used a stick at home, unless feeling self-conscious. Jordi went to help her up from her seat but she waved him away.

"Thank you. I can manage fine."

I followed them out onto the porch. Martha sat on a rocker writing a letter. Liz hobbled down the steps with Jordi at her elbow.

"Shall we start with the barn? It's simply the Eighth Wonder of the World."

"Sounds wondrous," Jordi said.

And they headed across the yard.

I sat in the rocker next to Martha and she looked up from her letter. "Henry?" I asked.

Martha nodded. "Do you have a message for him?"

"Just tell him I hope it's not too dull down there in Mobile with Farragut up here bombing Vicksburg."

Martha put down her pen and paper and watched as Liz and Jordi headed down the track toward the barn. "Liz has taken quite a liking to your friend."

"I think the feeling may be mutual."

"Do you? He seems a nice boy. I hope it's not just pity."

I sat up. "What a thing to say."

"Come on, Sam. Be realistic. Liz is a young woman now. Boys aren't exactly beating a path to the door."

"I guess not."

Martha looked away. "There again, pity would be preferable to nasty little pranks, like slipping a petite left-footed party shoe in her sewing bag."

"Who did that?" Martha had never mentioned this before, nor Liz.

"Do you really want to know?" she asked.

"Why not? I'll slap 'em silly."

"Even if I said it was Nancy Thurman?"

"I don't believe you."

Martha shrugged. "That's what Liz heard."

"It's just other girls gossiping. They're jealous of Nancy. Why would she do that?"

"Maybe 'cause she's cruel and two-faced like her mother."

I swung round to face her. "Nancy is nothing like her mother."

"And how would you know that, Sam? Just because she sweet-talked you a little? Or let you kiss her in the moonlight because it's wartime and you look handsome in a uniform? Don't be stupid."

"I'm not being stupid." Martha raised an eyebrow, but I persisted. "Nancy's not like that. I don't care what you heard."

"Fine. Think what you like, Sam. I just don't want you to get hurt. She's all but engaged to Frasier Melton."

"No, she's not. Frasier's in love with Bernice."

Martha sat up in her chair. "Bernice Thurman? Who-ate-all-the-cakes Bernice?"

"And on the topic of being cruel—"

"I'm sorry," Martha said. "But you can't believe that."

"I can believe whatever I like."

Martha held up her hands. "I don't want to argue about it, Sam. Not today."

So I sulked in silence as my sister went back to her letter, reaching over now and again to pat my arm. I was certain she must be wrong about Nancy. Women could be that way, going at each other like cats in a sack. But I decided there was no point in letting it spoil our morning. "Tell Henry this for me," I said to her. "Take it down exactly as I say: 'Save yourself! It's not too late!'"

"You mean from me?" She scribbled the words with a smile. "How droll. Henry'll like that."

~

That afternoon Cope drove Jordi and me back to town. I was sad to leave Sandhill, but I didn't dread the return to camp as much as I'd anticipated. Grandfather saw us off at the porch, but Martha and Liz walked along down to the gate. Liz gave Jordi a small roll of bonded paper tied with ribbon. It was a self-portrait done in pencil at her art lesson. She had signed it: "From your new friend."

"Terrible likeness, I know, but..." she said and turned away.

"Thank you," said Jordi. "It's beautiful."

"Come on, Autin. Let's get going before I lose my lunch," I said and climbed up into the buggy next to Cope.

Martha gave Jordi a kiss on the cheek, as did Liz, which made him blush bright red. He then hopped up back of the seat. Cope gave the reins a shake, and we drove away. Martha cried as always and waved until we rolled out of sight of the gate.

We arrived back at the shipyard by late afternoon and hurried to the galley. Bixby hadn't stopped drinking from the night before and was in a foul mood. He started in on Jordi the moment we reported for mess duty. Hearing that we'd spent the evening at Sandhill seemed to antagonize him even more.

"Hope you didn't disgrace yourself in front of them fine folk."

Jordi ignored him and prepared a tray with plates and cutlery for the officers' mess.

"Did they ask about your daddy? Hope not, seeing as how that'd be hard to answer in any certain way."

Wilson snorted a laugh.

Bixby took another pull on the half-pint bottle tucked in his apron. "So come on. Tell us about your evening," he taunted. "Did you recite some poetry? Do a dramatic reading? Or maybe just pull out that ragged newspaper and stumble through some old theater notice: Last night at the Apollo Mr. Simon Hays con-fuh... fuh...fuh... No Collins there to help with the big words."

Wilson laughed again. Bixby began to sharpen his kitchen knife. All the while, Jordi just kept polishing dinner forks, saying nothing.

"Did you tell them about old Sally? What a gal. Worked the best hotels in New Orleans 'til she got the pox. Did you show them the picture? My but she was a looker in her day. Hey, that rhymes: looker, hooker."

Not even Wilson laughed at this. Bixby snorted:

"Think the good reverend would have approved of old Sally?"

Jordi swung about. "Shut your filthy mouth!"

Bixby paused in his knife sharpening. "What did you say?"

Jordi met his gaze, for just an instant, and then bolted toward the door. The loaded mess tray clattered onto the floor. But Bixby caught his shirttail and threw him up against the wall.

"Where you going? Think you can speak to me like that, you little son of a whore?"

Jordi stopped struggling. He raised his chin and spat across Bixby's outstretched arm. The cook gave a murderous smile.

"So that's how it's gonna be." He slipped the knife into his back pocket and drove a fist into Jordi's gut. The boy dropped to the deck, the breath knocked out of him. "Seems last night has given you a few mistaken ideas." Bixby nudged him with the toe of his boot.

Jordi tucked himself into a ball, as though knowing what to expect. I stood transfixed, too afraid to move.

"Am I right?" Bixby said. "Answer me!"

But Jordi just lay there, quietly groaning. So Bixby kicked him hard in the small of the back. "Speak up!" he shouted and kicked him again in the head.

Wilson stood there aghast, unmoving. I had to do something. Bixby drew back for another kick, and I lurched forward to grab his collar. He stumbled off balance and fell on all fours, then twisted and lunged at me, pulling the kitchen knife from his back pocket.

"I'll gut you like a fish, boy."

Just then Read appeared in the galley with his pistol drawn. Four other soldiers rushed in behind.

"Drop that knife, Bixby, or I'll shoot you dead."

9

Bixby was arrested and locked in the hot, airless equipment shed that served as the brig. He faced a court-martial for his drunken conduct. Wilson took over in the galley and proved so bad a cook that Captain Brown faced a near mutiny. So within a few days Bixby was released and docked a month's wages. The captain pressed him into giving Jordi and me a halfhearted apology.

Over the next week the *Arkansas* remained at Yazoo City awaiting orders. Each day the river dropped just a little further down the bank with the dry summer weather, threatening to cut us off from the lower Yazoo and the Mississippi. It began to look as though we might stay upriver for the season—a prospect few welcomed. All week long my eyes kept straying to the river, to each snag that pocked out above the falling water level. My chances of seeing action were slowly draining away.

"Maybe they'd let us go back home until the fall, when the rains come," Albert whispered to me one evening as we lay in our bunks after lights-out. All the others were asleep. "Maybe we could even go back to school," he added.

I sat up. "School! Are you crazy?"

"Why not? I'm getting bored," said Albert. "And I doubt they'd miss us here."

"Go back to school and you'll damned well be missing me." I lay back on my scratchy mattress. "You sure get some queer notions."

But I too wondered how I'd last the summer.

∼

A shipment of over a hundred tins of regulation brown paint arrived one morning by steamer, free of charge from a supplier in Greenwood. So Eagan put us all on paint duty. The color was intended to make the boat blend into the tea brown hue of the Yazoo. But no matter how many coats we applied to the rail iron, the boat remained a rusty brown, a better color as it turned out. Yet it was terrible work with the heat and fumes.

Two days later I was ordered to report to the captain. I couldn't imagine why he'd want to see me. Both Lieutenant Read and Lieutenant Stevens were in his office on the *Capitol* when I knocked and entered. I stood and saluted in front of his desk.

"Stand at ease, Wood," he said and looked down at some papers on his desk. "Can you ride a horse?"

"Yes sir," I replied.

"How well do you know the Vicksburg Road?"

"Pretty well, as far as Haynes Bluff. I've cousins there."

"The Wickams? I know the family," said Read.

The captain frowned. "I've some important business in Vicksburg, which I've entrusted to Mr. Read here. He's asked for you to accompany him, seeing as you're also a local. It won't be an easy journey. You'll leave this evening, ride through the night. Do you think you're up to that?"

Read grinned. "Sure he is. Good Yazoo boy."

But I wasn't just so certain. The enemy was at Vicksburg.

Brown ignored Read and gave me a hard look. "So?"

"Yes sir. I'm up to it."

"That's the spirit," said Read. "Meet me in a half hour at the gate. Tell no one where you're going. Wear your civilian clothes but pack a fresh uniform. Don't want no farm boy sentry shooting us for Yankees in these blue jackets."

I went back to quarters and changed into my Sunday suit. I packed my one clean uniform into a satchel. Everyone was still on paint duty so I slipped away to avoid any questions. Anderson's boy from the livery in town waited at the gate with two saddled horses. Read arrived with a saddlebag over his shoulder and two gun belts. He handed one to me.

"Strap this on. Colt Navy. Ever shot one?"

I shook my head.

"Just pull back the hammer, point, and squeeze the trigger. Nothing to it. It's loaded and ready to fire, so try not to shoot your foot off. Hope we'll have no cause to use it."

I buckled on the stiff leather belt and felt the weight of the long pistol against my thigh. I climbed onto my mount, a glossy black mare named Jo. Read rode a large bay, far too tall for the lieutenant's short legs, but he managed to reach the saddle with help from Anderson's boy. The sun had dropped below the tree-tops by the time we rode out of town.

Read talked without stop for the first hour. He told me that Brown had been waiting weeks for orders from General Van Dorn in Vicksburg. The captain favored keeping the *Arkansas* upstream to protect the Yazoo river valley. He thought nothing would be gained fighting Farragut, and the South needed the provisions the Yazoo delta could supply. But he wanted to lay the option before Van Dorn and get an answer before it was too late.

"My call would be to steam down and give 'em hell," said Read. "But sadly I'm not in charge."

He pulled out a half-smoked cigar and lit up.

"Looking forward to meeting the general, though. Van Dorn is going places. You'd do well in Vicksburg to try and shake a few hands. Never know who might write a letter for you. Like I said before, it's all about who you know."

"So what attracted you to the navy?" I asked him. "A sense of duty?"

Read gave me a funny look.

"Hell no. Maybe. I don't know. Just good times. Get to sail round the world in a big damn ship with a fine bunch of boys. Fire cannons. Get drunk in Mexico. Hard work, of course, but nothing beats it in my book."

I had expected more of an answer than that. The way he talked, it seemed that it hardly mattered who we were fighting or killing. But that's all Read offered before he set off on some long tale about a cantina outside Mexico City. Eventually he grew tired of his own voice and we rode in silence. Night fell and a pale moon lit the road ahead, dusty and rutted. To our left rose the high, dark bluffs and to our right lay the river and the wide flat delta beyond.

I wondered why Read had chosen me to accompany him, why he seemed to favor me so. We had almost nothing in common beyond geography. Did he see me as some young, eager version of himself? Nothing could be further from the truth. Even my place on the crew was based on a lie. Why would I want a career in the navy? What had naval life done for my father?

Hours went by and we met no one on that empty road as we rode past farms and villages: Crupp, Satartia, Germania, Eldorado. All the windows in the houses were dark. Sometime in the early hours of morning I was awakened by Read poking me in the ribs with the barrel of his pistol.

"Sorry. Dozed off," I said.

He put a finger to his lips. Out across a narrow field of corn the Yazoo River ran black in the moonlight. Midstream a Union ironclad gunboat lay anchored, its lanterns reflected in the still water, four dark cannon barrels pointing toward us from its casemate. A sentry stood on the upper spar deck, a musket across his chest, looking out in our direction. Read jumped from his horse and motioned toward a stand of trees on the bluff side of the road. I climbed down from my saddle, took the mare's bridle, and led her into the brush.

For two hundred yards or so we struggled in the darkness through briars and tangled undergrowth before Read felt it safe to take to the road again. We then cantered a good two miles before slowing to a trot.

"That was a different boat from the one that fired on us below Satartia," said Read. "Looked like an ironclad from the Union upriver fleet. If the *Arkansas* meets her, it'll be a stand-up fight."

The rest of that long night passed in a tired blur. Just after sunrise we reached the outskirts of Vicksburg where the road cut up into the bluffs toward the city. We'd covered more than forty miles in one night.

A sentry stopped us at the outskirts and directed us to the headquarters of a Colonel Withers of the 1st Mississippi Light Artillery. We rode up a hard dirt track off the main road to a small wooden house on the crest of a bluff. Tents crowded the small yard. Further up the hill a row of gun emplacements had been dug into the bluff. Howitzers and Napoleon cannons were aimed out over the Yazoo Road below. Smoke rose from a dozen mess fires and the air smelled of bacon and coffee.

A stable boy took our horses for a feed and rest. Read went into the house to call on the colonel. I sat on the front steps, unable to keep my eyes open. It seemed only seconds later that Read nudged me with the toe of his boot.

"Come on. Let's get some breakfast."

We were led into a small dining room at the back of the house. Two officers sat at the oak table reading newspapers over their breakfast. An orderly brought us plates of bacon and scrambled eggs and hominy grits with hot mugs of coffee. Few meals had tasted so good to me.

Just as I finished my eggs an odd whistling sound came from the open window. Both of the officers looked up from their papers with mild interest. The sound grew louder, like a scream, and ended in a deep thud that rattled the china and silverware in the sideboard. I pushed out my chair in panic and crouched down, ready to jump under the table.

"Keep your seat, boy," said one of the officers. "Weren't that close. That'll be the Yankee mortar crews upriver announcing they've finished their breakfast."

Read grinned down at me. I climbed back in my chair and tried not to appear concerned when the next shell came whistling in not a minute later. All morning the Yankees pounded the bluffs, though no one seemed to pay much mind except me. Read found this amusing and took to shouting "Boom!" at unexpected moments just to watch me jump.

An orderly showed us to a small bedroom up the stairs and brought us a basin of hot water to wash and shave. He took away our uniforms to be pressed. Read lay out on the bed and fell instantly asleep. I spread a blanket on a rag rug on the floor and used my suit coat as a pillow, but found it hard to sleep, what with Read's snoring and the regular rumble of the falling mortar shells.

Later that morning Colonel Withers arranged for a buggy to take us to General Van Dorn's headquarters in town. Read wore his old formal U.S. Navy uniform: blue peaked cap and wool long coat with two rows of brass buttons, gold epaulettes, and trim on the cuffs. Blue trousers with a sword and scabbard at the belt completed the outfit. He certainly looked impressive. I didn't feel too shabby either in my blue shirt and bell-bottoms.

Vicksburg did not appear much like a city besieged as we drove through the streets. People thronged the sidewalks, hurrying in and out of shops; children played in a schoolyard. But on the corner of Crawford Street we came across one house half in ruins. A gable end had been blown away and a bedroom with an ornate fireplace and flowered wallpaper lay open to the sky. Our driver told us a stray mortar shell had struck the house, killing a nursemaid and an eight-year-old girl.

Crawford Street ran steeply up the bluff and was

lined with grand houses. We stopped in front of a large two-story mansion with more than a dozen horses tied to the gallery porch. Read presented himself to the guard on duty and was shown in to wait in the parlor. I found a rocking chair in the shade of the porch and sat and watched soldiers bustle in and out with orders and reports.

The house had a commanding view of the river. Not a single steamboat or tug or barge passed before the city. One of the busiest waterways in the world, choked lifeless by the Federal siege.

Half an hour later Read strode out the door. "Come on, Wood. We're done here."

The buggy took us back to Withers's headquarters. Read said nothing the entire journey. The colonel himself met us on the porch of the farmhouse.

"See that the horses are saddled," Read said to me and disappeared inside with Withers. I went to the stable and found the groom. Ten minutes later I brought the horses round. Read stood on the steps talking to one of Withers's officers, a tall wild-haired lieutenant named Bassett. I had no idea what was going on, what General Van Dorn had said in the short meeting.

"Go up and get our gear," Read said. "Lieutenant Bassett here is taking us upriver for a look-see, and then we're heading back to Yazoo City."

The three of us rode north of town on a narrow path that cut through dense wood along the riverbank. At some points the path grew so entangled with vines and briars we had to dismount. But soon we reached our objective, and Bassett used his sword to cut a path to the edge of the thicket for a view out over the Mississippi.

Upriver, anchored in a line along the east bank, lay Farragut's fleet of thirteen heavy sloops of war, massive ocean-going steamships with towering masts stripped of sail for river duty. Moored to the bending west bank above us was the Federal upriver fleet of Commodore Davis, more than thirty ironclad gunboats and rams and another thirty or so mortar boats. Among them were countless other tugs and barges, troop transports, and hospital ships.

My heart beat wildly; my mouth grew dry. I felt as though I was standing on the edge of some perilous cliff, seeing for the first time the full might of the enemy stretched out across the horizon. A jolt of fear and despair shot down my spine. How could we possibly face such a force with just the *Arkansas*?

Read surveyed the scene with his field glass and scribbled details in a small notebook.

"Have a look," said Bassett, passing me his field glass. "See the big three-master at the head? That's Farragut's ship, the USS *Hartford*."

I trained the glasses on the massive warship with its tangle of rigging, its long deck covered in white canvas awnings. Twenty-four guns I counted: ten on the facing broadside and another ten opposite, I assumed, with two more on the bow and stern—more than twice the fire power of the *Arkansas*.

Read suddenly snatched my collar and yanked me back into the thicket. A launch boat with a dozen or so sailors from one of the ships was rowing along the bank not twenty yards from us. We sat silently and listened to their shouts and the *thunk, thunk* of the oars as they passed, unaware of being watched.

"Well, I've seen more than I care to," Read whispered and turned back toward the horses.

Bassett guided us to the Yazoo Road, and it was after nightfall before we started on the long return journey. Read pushed the horses hard down the moonlit road and said nothing of his discussion with Van Dorn or the orders. By Haynes Bluff my curiosity had got the better of me. When we stopped to water the horses at the town pump, I asked him direct: Was the *Arkansas* going to stay upriver like Captain Brown wanted?

Read looked annoyed. "Why are you asking that? Didn't you sign up to fight Yankees?"

"Well...yes sir."

"Good," he replied. "'Cause fight Yankees is what we're gonna do."

He then told me what Van Dorn had written in the sealed order tucked inside his jacket. I couldn't believe what I was hearing. The *Arkansas* was to sail down the Yazoo to the Mississippi and fight her way through the Federal fleet before landing at Vicksburg. From there she was to head downriver and attack the mortar schooners and ships below town before proceeding to New Orleans and out the lower passes into the Gulf of Mexico to the port of Mobile to raise the Federal blockade!

"And that's just before breakfast," Read added grimly. "It's absurd. Van Dorn's a fool."

He climbed back into his saddle and yanked the big bay up from the trough. "But by damn, Wood, we'll see some action."

~

I wished then I hadn't asked the question, nor even been to Vicksburg to see what I'd seen. The reality was too hard to bear. Neither of us spoke much for the rest of the journey. I turned things over and over in my mind. Plenty could happen before we made it downriver. The *Arkansas* could run aground at Satartia with the falling river level. The engines could fail. Captain Brown could protest the orders. Anyone would agree it was a suicide mission, being so outnumbered.

Or was it? The *Arkansas* was certainly no ordinary ship. Encased in armor above the waterline, not vulnerable like wooden ships, a big safe iron cocoon from which we'd blast away at the fleet. Whatever shells hit us would just bounce off like summer rain. I tried to push all other possible outcomes from my head.

Toward the early hours of morning I fell into an exhausted trance with the motion of the saddle. I had fretful dreams of large looming ships, cannons belching fire, shells screaming overhead, black water filling the gun deck, no escape.

Midshipman Wikers met us at Liverpool Landing just before daybreak. Read handed over the orders for Wikers to take on to Yazoo City. We rented a room at a cheap hotel by the wharf. My mattress was full of bedbugs but I slept like a dead man. Ten hours later I awoke in a sweat and went for some air at the open window. There above the river barrier, moored to the levee, lay the *Arkansas*. She had already steamed down from Yazoo City while we slumbered.

~

Next morning I was back onboard. We waited while a detail of men under the command of Lieutenant Gift cleared a passage through the log barrier across the river. The army engineer from Jackson who designed the barrier had claimed it couldn't be removed inside of a week. Gift's crew, working only with axes and a small charge of powder, had the *Arkansas* through in less than an hour. The crew cheered as we steamed past Liverpool Landing. Spirits were high after the long wait in Yazoo City.

I tried to avoid Albert and the rest of the boys that day. Read had sworn me to secrecy and I knew they'd press me for answers.

We sailed the few miles to the river bar at Satartia. James Shacklett from the river steamer *Era* had the wheel, no better pilot on the Yazoo. He eased the *Arkansas* into the deep water under the cut bank at Satartia and ran clear of the bar without breaking a sweat. There we moored and spent the rest of the day at gunnery drill.

That night we took mess out on the bank in a swarm of mosquitoes. Word had spread about the orders from Van Dorn, and Jordi began to interrogate me.

"Come on. What's waiting for us down there?"

"I'm not supposed to say."

"We won't tell."

"I can't. It's orders."

"More than a rowboat, less than the Spanish Armada?"

The twins laughed, but not Albert. He'd been quiet all evening. Just then he stood up and tossed the remnants of his coffee into the fire.

"Listen to you," he snapped. "Talking about orders like some kind of officer. You're just a boy rating like us. Remember?"

Jordi and the twins looked away, and I realized this wasn't the first time they'd discussed my trip with Read to Vicksburg.

"I never pretended to be anything else," I replied.

But Albert just shook his head and walked off down the bank.

"What's your problem?" I called after him. "I'm only doing as told."

He ignored me and kept on walking.

"Come on. Stop!" I shouted and ran after him. "Where you going?"

Suddenly he swung around to face me. "Are we going to die, Sam? Give me a straight answer. No crap."

"What kind of question is that?"

"A big one."

Albert looked me square in the eye. It wasn't fair, but neither was my answer.

"How should I know? What do you want to hear?"

"The truth. Is that too much to ask?"

He turned away and headed back toward camp. A sudden rush of hatred rose inside me, and I found myself wishing he'd just stayed home in Yazoo City.

That afternoon the paymaster passed me a letter that had been left at the shipyard gate. I kept it in my pocket, waiting for a private moment. The writing on the envelope was neat and confident.

Samuel James Wood, Esquire

Tucked inside was a short letter along with a fine lace-trimmed linen handkerchief, hardly larger than the palm of my hand.

Dearest Sam,

I am sorry that circumstances have not allowed us time to better develop our "friendship." Time seems a rare commodity in these troubled days. I remember fondly (and will always) our walk along the river and how handsome you looked in your uniform. You do the South great credit (even if others in my family do not agree). Now is the time for bravery: yours loud and active, amidst the rumble of cannon; mine patient and prayerful. Tears fall as I write, but I will dry them and be strong for you and your shipmates. Such are the sacrifices we make for our great fledgling nation. Enclosed is a small remembrance of me. Use it to wipe your brow in the fever of battle. May it bring you faith and courage.

Take care my love,
Nancy

Over the next days I re-read that letter so many times I could recite its contents. I agonized over every word, every mark on the page. I even searched the paper for signs of her falling tears (and found none). I kept it tucked in my trouser pocket, along with the small lace handkerchief, which smelled vaguely of rosewater.

Next morning—Monday, July 14—the *Arkansas* fired her two engines. Shacklett eased out mid-river below Satartia bar and headed downstream. A near disaster, however, delayed our progress. Just before noon Milliken discovered that a steam leak from one of the boilers had breached the forward magazine and wet the powder supply. We had to land at a sawmill along the bank and spread the powder on canvas tarps to dry in the hot sun. This took most of the day. It was nearly midnight by the time we reached the landing at Haynes Bluff.

Vicksburg now lay but a few hours sailing. Each man knew what was to be faced that next day, so there was little rest among the crew that night. Bixby broke out cold rations—salt pork and hardtack—and brewed urns of strong, hot coffee. Lanterns burned low on the gun deck. Some men tried to sleep; others wrote letters or played cards or draughts. I wandered around the boat pouring coffee for my shipmates, grateful to be doing something—anything—to take my mind off what was to come that dawn.

Later I found Jordi in a corner of the gun deck. The twins lay nearby, dozing on bedrolls. Albert was sleeping up on the spar deck. We'd hardly exchanged a word since last night. Jordi didn't see me approach, and I noticed he had Liz's self-portrait resting on the open newspaper in his lap. He closed it quickly when he saw me and shoved it under his jacket.

"You tired?" I asked him.

"Not really," he replied.

"Me neither."

So we found a deck of cards and played until three in the morning, when Hollins appeared with his drum to rouse the crew.

10

Dawn that morning found the *Arkansas* about seven miles from the confluence of the Mississippi. Just ahead the Yazoo broadened into a small lake formed by a cutoff channel of the Mississippi known locally as "Old River." The air was warm and calm, and a dense black plume rose from our funnel high over the trees, signaling our presence to anyone who cared to notice.

Sunlight streamed through the open ports and the lanterns were extinguished. Guns had been loaded and primed and the crews stood by, ready for orders. Coal heavers below fed the boilers, making the heat on board ever more hellish. Most men had stripped off shirts and were bare to the waist with handkerchiefs bound round their heads. Officers removed their uniform coats and stood in undershirts.

Surgeon Hix had served out tourniquets to the division officers with instructions for use. He now waited below in the berth deck with his gleaming instruments and rolls of lint laid out on long tables.

Sand had been sprinkled across the gun deck to prevent men slipping in blood. Division tubs between the guns had been filled with fresh drinking water, and fire buckets had been put in place. Spare breechings and tools to service the cannons waited in chests and were stored in racks. Cutlasses and pistols were strapped on. Rifles were loaded and bayonets fixed.

Down in the lower decks men lined the passages to pass powder, shell, and shot from the magazines and shell rooms up the forward ladder to Quartermaster Eagan at the hatchway. There Albert and I and the twins would deliver it across the crowded gun deck to our divisions. All was ready for action and there was hardly a sound apart from the dull *thump, thump* of the turning propellers.

Captain Brown waited with Lieutenant Stevens atop the casemate, his marine glass trained on the river ahead. Soon after daylight they spotted three plumes of smoke rising over the trees a few miles downriver. The captain had no doubt it was the enemy. He climbed down the main ladder way, and Stevens called together the crew, who crowded onto the gun deck.

Brown stood by the pilothouse platform between the two forward Columbiad cannons, wearing his full-dress uniform. He pulled out a handkerchief to wipe the sweat from his brow.

"Gentlemen!" he shouted. "In seeking combat as we now do, we must win or perish."

Albert shifted on his feet next to me. I felt suddenly

dizzy and had to lean back on the ladder to steady myself.

"Should I fall, whoever succeeds to the command will do so with the resolution to go through the enemy's fleet, or go to the bottom. Should they carry us by boarding, the ship must be blown up. On no account must it fall into the hands of the enemy. Go to your guns."

We answered with cheers and cries of "Hurrah!"

I moved into position with my gun division. I peeked out through the narrow forward port and saw nothing ahead but open river. Gun Captain Tanner barked orders and positioned his gun crew, which included both the older Conroy brothers. Dermot manned the tackle that opened and closed the heavy iron gun-port shutter. Thomas, a red-faced bull of a man, was sponger on the broadside Dahlgren. Big Wallace also worked Lieutenant Gift's division as a side-tackle man on the four-ton Columbiad, utilizing his size and strength to pull the heaving ropes that ran the heavy gun out on its rails for firing. His pal Hector was working as a loader on one of Read's stern rifles.

Lieutenant Stevens moved among the crews with words of encouragement as the gun captains shouted last-minute instructions. I felt my stomach churn with too much coffee and no breakfast. I bent over and tried not to be sick. Just then I caught Wallace's eye. He grinned at me with excitement.

A cry rose from the pilothouse. "Enemy off the port bow!"

THE PASSAGE

No one on the gun deck had a clear view, but just rounding a bend a mile or so distant, three Federal boats appeared in a line abreast, steaming upriver at full power. Forward and center was the large, twin-stacked, thirteen-gun ironclad Read and I had passed on the river that night we rode to Vicksburg. She was named the *Carondelet,* one of the 'Pook's turtles' designed especially for river fighting. The vessel lay low in the water, with slanting armored sides just like ours. To the left flank was an eight-gun timberclad steamer called the *Tyler* and to the right the unarmed ram, *Queen of the West.*

No doubt the *Arkansas* had long been spotted. Forward we pressed, engines rumbling. No one spoke, apart from a few whispered instructions. Gift leaned with his back to the Columbiad, head bowed, chewing at a rag nail on his finger. Tanner peered down the cannon barrel through the bow port, trying to glimpse the enemy. Somewhere in the lower decks Barbot's dog barked incessantly. Minutes passed like hours. I clenched my teeth and tried to hold down the panic, to take one breath after another. I just wanted it to start, to be done with the waiting.

Just then we heard a muffled *boom.* An instant later the boat shuddered with a deafening thud, like from the blow of a giant sledgehammer. The shot had struck the front shield, but the rail iron held and the projectile bounded away over the top of the casemate. Two more shells slammed into the armor near our front port and shattered into hot fragments that whistled through the air.

No one on the gun deck had yet to see the enemy. Dermot Conroy sat crouched, holding his tackle rope by the forward broadside port.

"Where are the bastards?" he muttered to no one in particular and leaned out the opening for a quick look.

I heard more shots, and just then Dermot's body slammed against the edge of the port in a spray of blood. He fell backward onto the deck at my feet, missing most of the top half of his skull. A cannon bolt had careened off the side of the *Arkansas* and struck him full in the face. Blood spread in a wide pool from the twisted corpse.

I backed away in horror. Lieutenant Stevens sprang forward and grabbed Dermot's legs. He shouted to the nearest man for help. "Come on. Get it overboard. Can't have this lying on deck."

But the man nearest to him was Thomas.

"I can't do it, sir!" he cried. "That's my brother."

Tanner shoved Thomas aside, took Dermot by the arms and flung the body out the port into the river. Stevens dumped a bucket of sand and quickly kicked it over the blood. I watched all this in breathless disbelief. It was just so sudden and so completely brutal.

Thomas stood quietly sobbing, still clutching his sponge staff. The twins didn't even know then it was their brother who'd been hit.

Shells continued to hammer on the iron casemate. I stood transfixed, unable to move. Some of Dermot's blood had splashed onto my boot, but I couldn't bring myself to wipe it off. All I wanted to do was run.

I heard Eagan holler, "Wood! Back to your post."

But his voice seemed far away. He hollered again. I looked up and he saw the panic in my face. His expression hardened.

"Shift it, boy, or I'll throw *you* out that port."

I stumbled back to my post. Lieutenant Gift eased up behind me and laid a hand on my shoulder. "Hold fast," he said quietly.

Not a single shot had yet been fired from the *Arkansas*. Our bow guns could not be brought to bear on the approaching boats, owing to the slight curve in the river. Both the *Tyler* and the *Carondelet* kept up steady fire with their bow guns. Down below, our engines pounded at full steam and the gap between us closed fast. I overheard Tanner comment to Gift: "Looks like we're gonna ram." The pointed iron prow of the *Arkansas* could punch a hole in the thickest wooden hull.

Seeing us approach at speed, the middle ironclad inexplicably backed engines to turn and retreat downstream. The other two Federals then did the same. Brown ordered the pilot to steer for the *Tyler*.

Just as the timberclad made the turn, her stern moved across the sights of our bow cannons. Gift shouted "Fire!" and yanked his lanyard cord. The big Columbiad roared. Smoke filled the air, alight with bright orange flame. The cannon screeched back on its rails. Upon hitting the wooden chocks, its heavy barrel recoiled off the carriage and tumbled with a crack onto the deck, nearly crushing one of the crew. The shell screamed over the water and tore into the *Tyler*'s wooden hull, exploding deep in her bowels. Yet the Federal timberclad still made the turn and opened again on us with her stern guns as her big side-wheel paddles churned away, taking her further downstream.

It took ten minutes for Gift's crew to set up the winch and hoist the heavy Columbiad barrel back onto its carriage. Meanwhile the other bow Columbiad pounded away at the fleeing Federals. A Texan named McCalla, reckoned to be the best gunner onboard, captained the crew, who worked with steady precision: fire, recoil, load, run-out, fire.

Albert stood by the forward hatch clutching his pass box, his face gray and dripping with sweat. Lieutenant Barbot shouted for extra ordinance for his rear broadside cannon. Eagan hauled up a 32-pound solid iron shot and gave it to Albert to take over to the loader. Albert clutched the iron ball in both hands, but in pushing past the pilothouse platform, he stumbled over the gun rails and dropped it with a loud thud on the oak planking. Eagan blistered him with curses as Albert chased the ball rolling across the deck.

Heavy bolts and shells from the enemy's stern guns bent and warped the rail iron armor, but still did not penetrate. Lieutenant Gift shouted at me to fetch an 8-inch shell with a 5-second fuse. I ran to the hatch and repeated the order to Eagan, who bellowed it below. Just then I heard the captain shout for Stevens to ready the starboard guns. Sparks and iron fragments shattering against the front shield filled the air above the *Arkansas*, yet Captain Brown remained up top the casemate directing the action, fully exposed.

Out in the river the *Queen of the West* had peeled off to the right, as though maneuvering into position to ram us. Brown ordered a "turn to port" and the *Arkansas* veered, bringing her starboard guns to bear. Lieutenant Stevens shouted "Fire!" and a three-gun broadside rocked the ship, knocking me off my feet. Missiles flew low over the water and crashed through the Federal ram's hull. Her captain had a change of heart and steered the ram downriver to race ahead and warn the fleet of our coming.

Acrid smoke filled the casemate. Tears streamed down my cheeks. My heart pounded in my chest, but I felt much better doing something—relaying powder and shell as it passed up the hatch. Another salvo hit the front shield, and I heard a clatter behind me. I turned just in time to see Captain Brown tumble backward down the main ladder way. He sat up on the deck and reached to his head. Lieutenant Stevens ran to his side. Brown pulled away a bloodied hand and held it out for inspection. "See any brains?" he asked.

"No sir," Stevens replied.

"Good. Help me up."

Seconds later another shell struck the *Arkansas*. Smoke and flame burst from the pilothouse as it tore through the armor and blasted away half the wheel. Fire crews rushed in to clear the debris and douse the flames. The shot had killed Chief Pilot Hughes and wounded Shacklett, as well as a young Virginia seaman named Pearson. A Mississippi pilot—James Brady—took charge of the shattered wheel.

The *Arkansas* had now drawn within musket range of the *Tyler*. Sharpshooters on the Union boat's upper decks fired in volleys, aiming for our open ports and at Captain Brown, now back atop the shield. Minie balls ricocheted about the gun deck. Midshipman Wikers fell with a shot to his thigh but refused to leave his station. A medical orderly bandaged the wound as best he could, and Wikers limped back to his gun.

Ahead the ironclad *Carondelet* now paddled for dear life. McCalla's gun had pierced her thin armor at least four times. Having the advantage of speed, Brown now intended to use our bow ram.

Lieutenant Gift had his forward gun back in commission now, firing like clockwork. I stumbled back and forth from the hatch with shell and powder. Standing by for orders, I managed a brief glimpse down the barrel of the Columbiad. A sailor stood loading a cannon on a stern port sill of the *Carondelet*. I could make out every feature of his face; we were now that close. Just then Gift pulled his lanyard cord. I plugged my ears and looked again when the smoke had cleared. Nothing remained of the man or the gun but a splintered hole.

The *Carondelet* steamed toward willows growing along the eastern bank of the Old River. Her steering appeared to be shot away, and she was listing badly.

Brady shouted up to the captain that to follow risked running the *Arkansas* into the mud.

Brown ignored the warning and gave the order: "Hard aport and depress guns."

Crews along the port side ran up the elevator screws on their cannons so that the barrels were aimed down into the water. Brady swung the helm, and the *Arkansas* ran up alongside the *Carondelet* so close as to almost touch. Stevens hollered "Fire!" and a deafening three-gun broadside crashed into the enemy boat's timbers at the waterline. The *Arkansas* rolled deeply with the recoil, taking water over the deck opposite.

The *Carondelet* drifted into weeds along the bank, badly damaged and out of action. Only the shallow, muddy bottom kept her from sinking. A wild cheer rose from the gun deck. Gift allowed himself a smile as he peered out the port ahead to try and catch sight of the other enemy boats. Brady then turned the *Arkansas* back downstream and gave Read a chance to use his two stern rifles. They exploded with a parting salvo that tore again into the stricken ironclad.

My ears ached and my clothes were soaked through with sweat, yet relief spread over me like a cooling breeze. I looked for Albert. He stood by the forward ladder, bent over and breathing hard, hands on knees, his face blackened with powder.

"You okay?" I asked.

He looked up, wide-eyed with shock, uncomprehending. I then noticed Thomas and the twins. They stood and stared aghast at the bloody gun port from which their brother had been thrown.

"Conroys!" Eagan shouted across the gun deck.

All three turned.

"Time for that later. Get back to your stations."

~

Far downriver the *Tyler* raced ahead of us, firing an occasional shot from her stern rifle. Captain Brown made a tour of the boat to inspect damages. Ship's carpenters went to work on the pilothouse, bolting boilerplate over the shell breech. Down in the engine and fire rooms, temperatures had reached upwards of one hundred-twenty degrees. Stevens organized relief parties from the crew and rotated men in and out every fifteen minutes. The ship's funnel, being so riddled with cannon shot and minie balls, resembled a nutmeg grater. This caused the furnace to lose draft and lowered the steam pressure in the boilers. Our engines could make no better than four knots.

An iron fragment had pierced our division tub and drinking water spilled across the deck. Eagan shouted for me to get the hole plugged and fetch more water. I begged some caulk putty off one of the carpenters and took a bucket below to the galley.

Surgeon Hix had Pearson stretched out on a bloody mess table under a dim lantern. Two orderlies held him down as the doctor prepared his instruments. A ragged wound tore across his shoulder and splintered bone poked through the flesh of his upper arm. I looked away. On the next table lay Hughes's body, covered in blood-soaked canvas. Wikers sat in a chair waiting his turn with the other wounded, his face now gray with pain from the gunshot to his thigh.

A canvas screen had been hung across the far end of the deck. Behind it Bixby sat in a chair with his boots propped up on the galley station. Wilson stood before the stove, brewing coffee.

"I see you survived," he said as I hung my bucket over the water pump. Hix had begun his work with the bone saw, producing a hideous grating sound. Pearson screamed; he had nothing more to ease the pain than a leather bite strap.

"Damn shame about Conroy," Bixby shouted over the noise. "But then at least we don't have to listen to that damn Irish whistle no more."

Bixby grinned up at Wilson, who seemed not to hear. He was grimly watching his pots. I filled my bucket without reply. Pearson had by then fallen unconscious. I pushed back through the canvas screen to return top deck. Hix had the arm off just below the shoulder, sewing together skin flaps at the stump. I'd seen more than enough for one day. But the sun had hardly cleared the horizon; that terrible day had only just begun.

~

Soon the Mississippi opened out broad before us as we passed the mouth of the Yazoo. Both enemy boats had raced out of sight. Ten miles of river lay between us and the safety of the Confederate guns above Vicksburg—and in that gap waited an entire enemy fleet.

We swung into the current, and Stevens ordered the beat to quarters. Out the ports the Mississippi seemed immense compared to the muddy Yazoo. I took my position again beside Thomas, who stood grim and silent. Our speed increased with the swift current. Soon we rounded Tuscumbia Bend, and the Federals came into view.

Tanner peered out of his gun port. "Sweet Jesus," he muttered.

Each man in each crew craned his neck for a glimpse through the narrow ports. Just then I heard Lieutenant Stevens shouting my name. "Take some water up top the shield. Captain's thirsty," he ordered. "And come straight back."

So I grabbed a bucket and ladle and climbed up the ladder to the open sky. Bright sunlight glared off the river ahead. My eyes took a moment to adjust after the gloom below. Captain Brown stood alone at the very front of the shield atop the pilothouse. I can hardly do justice to the vista that lay less than a mile or so distant. There before me stood a forest of masts and smokestacks. Dozens of vessels of every description—gunboats, sloops of war, ironclads, mortar ketches, converted river steamers—lined both banks, all bristling with cannon. On the Louisiana side of the river lay the camp of the Federal Army, over three thousand strong, row upon row of white canvas tents.

I could see soldiers pushing field artillery up along the levee to join the firing line.

My legs wobbled like India rubber. I spilled most of the water from the bucket as I climbed out onto the deck where Captain Brown stood.

"Wood! Come join me." Blood crusted his beard, and hair stuck out wildly from the cotton bandage that had been wrapped tightly about his head like a turban. He smiled with pleasure, calm as a millpond. I handed him the ladle. He took a deep swallow.

"Much better," he said and looked back to the river. "What a grand sight. See that big sloop to the left? That's the USS *Richmond,* commanded by Andy Cummings, one of my former midshipmen."

I waited desperately for him to hand back the ladle so I could be dismissed and duck back below.

But he took another sip. "Lord, what havoc we could do with a real ram."

Ahead I could see enemy ironclads getting up steam to attack. I heard the whistle of bullets from sharpshooters on the shore. Lead slugs began to ping off the side of the casemate. I ducked my head but Brown remained upright, giving the firing no notice. I wondered if maybe his wound had made him deranged. He certainly looked mad, staring out from under the bloody turban.

"We could certainly have used your father's gunnery skills today. Just a duck shoot out there. Fire in any direction and hit a mark."

Only then did he seem to notice how I crouched at

his side. "Sorry, Wood. Best head back below."

Just as he finished his sentence, a bullet shattered the marine glass in his other hand. "Damn," he cried with mild annoyance, as if he'd dropped a teacup doing the washing up.

"Thank you, sir," I said hastily, snatching the ladle. I dashed back to the hatch and left him shaking broken glass out of the brass tubing. I slid down the ladder and pushed back through the crew into position.

Thomas looked up at me with a pale expression. "What's it like out there?"

"You don't want to know," I replied.

On we steamed toward the waiting guns. I heard Captain Brown shout to Brady at the wheel: "Shave that line of men-of-war as close as you can."

Brady steered the *Arkansas* in close toward the big warships anchored off the left bank. In behind them the few Federal rams that had managed to raise steam waited, ready to dash out and strike us. Brown was determined to give them no headway.

A steady hail of musketry rained against the iron casemate. All onboard waited for the full storm to break upon us. Lieutenant Gift crouched again by the big Columbiad, peering out the forward port. He suddenly guffawed. Just what could be funny was beyond imagining.

"Hurry and fetch Mr. Read!" he shouted to me. "Tell him we've an old friend come to call."

I dashed back to the stern and gave Read the message. He followed me at ease, swinging his primer lanyard. Ahead of the *Arkansas* the first Federal vessel had swung into the river to engage us. It was a twin-masted steam gunboat with No. 6 painted on her funnel, the very same ship that Read had sworn to sink for killing his captain on the *McRae* above the forts at New Orleans.

Just as we reached the forward station the gunboat fired her bow pivot gun. A ring of white smoke billowed out toward us, and grape shot sprayed across the water, intended for our open ports. But her gunner had aimed too low.

Brady touched the starboard helm sharply, and the No. 6 appeared in the Columbiad's sights. Gift yanked the lanyard and the cannon discharged, sending a shell crashing into the gunboat's bow. Stevens ordered the port guns ready, and, passing close, the *Arkansas* fired a broadside that splintered into the vessel's hull. The No. 6 made no attempt to follow us. Read smiled like a cat with cream and went back to his post.

Almost as though in answer to the insult, over a hundred guns suddenly opened on us from all sides. Iron shot and shell battered off the casemate in a continuous roar like a summer hailstorm on a tin roof. Hot fragments and grape sang through the open ports, ricocheting across the gun deck. Huge columns of water sprayed up from the river where the cannon shots fell short of aim. All ten guns on the *Arkansas* roared to life.

So calm was the day that smoke from the cannon fire settled thickly on the river. Our gunners at times had only the muzzle flashes of the enemy to direct their aim. But as we advanced it hardly mattered. The line of fire from Federal ships had grown into a circle, completely enclosing us. Our gunners could aim at any point of the compass without fear of missing the enemy.

I had little time to think about any of this. Back and forth I dodged, clattering against men and guns with my pass box, feeding my crew powder and munitions.

Eagan directed operations, bawling instructions down the hatch. "Nine-inch shell, 5-second fuse." And then he would pass it up to me. "Here, lad. Mind you don't drop the bastard."

Acrid smoke choked the air such that I could scarcely breathe or see through my tears. Broadside cannons in constant action roared back and recoiled against groaning breech ropes. To take one misstep risked being crushed to death. So intense grew the hurricane of missiles rattling against our shields that the glass shattered in the gun deck lanterns. Water danced and splashed out of the division tubs. Still the armor held.

Downriver another Federal steamed out from behind one of the large warships, intent on ramming us. But she was too slow in making the turn upstream.

"Go through him, Brady!" Captain Brown shouted from atop the shield.

The pilot called down the speaking tube to the engineer asking for full power on the engines. He steered the *Arkansas*'s iron prow toward the Federal ram. But Lieutenant Gift got her in the sight of his Columbiad first and yanked the lanyard. An 8-inch shell screamed low over the water and tore into the Federal's hull, exploding in her boiler. Clouds of scalding hot steam burst from the hatches. Men scrambled onto deck howling in agony, tearing off their shirts and leaping into the river. The Federal drifted midstream, and the *Arkansas* sliced past her, straight through the mass of drowning sailors.

Just beyond, we drew abreast of a large sloop of war. A stocky Missourian gun loader named Faulkner shouted to me for powder when the big sloop let go a massive broadside. A heavy shot struck our side above the bow gun. The concussion hurled Faulkner into the side of the Columbiad. He stood up, rubbing his hip.

"Bastards!" he shouted to me. "Least ways they hardly ever strike twice in the same place."

I grinned wanly and bent down to the hatch to retrieve more munitions. Two seconds later a shell entered the breech made by the first shot and exploded in our bulwark. I was knocked flat by the force of the blast. My ears rang, and I choked on the dense black smoke that filled the gun deck.

Not a soul remained standing at the forward Columbiad. I stumbled back astern and nearly tripped over Wallace. The big man lay on deck with his right leg blown clear off. Blood soaked through his undershirt from a hole in his chest. He looked up at me with fearful, pleading eyes. I had no idea what to do. I shouted for a medical orderly and reached into my pocket. All I could find was Nancy Thurman's handkerchief. I pressed it to the wound on his chest. It soaked through in an instant. Wallace rolled his eyes back once and then forward again, blank and staring. I kept shouting, though I knew he was dead.

"Leave him be, Wood, and get me some powder," Gift snarled as he sat up among the debris.

His face was black and bloodied, his beard half singed off. Sixteen men, including Faulkner and Tanner, had been killed or wounded by that shell. Only Gift and Quartermaster Curtis remained fit for duty from that entire gun crew. Lieutenant Stevens ran to the engine hatch and grabbed a fire hose. Soon he'd extinguished the flames burning in the cotton-bale lining of the bulwark.

By now the roar of the bombardment was deafening. I returned with the powder as ordered and helped Gift and Curtis reload the Columbiad. A second shell then burst through the casemate in a shower of iron and wooden splinters. I was thrown forward and struck my head on the front bulwark. I felt a searing pain in my shoulder. Gift rose up, clutching his arm in agony. The shell had pierced just above the broadside gun port and had struck down every man at the forward Dahlgren. Thomas Conroy was killed outright. The shell had then sailed across the deck and punched a hole through the smokestack before crashing among one of the stern gun crews.

Ahead of the *Arkansas* a large ironclad pushed out into the river to block our way. Brown ordered the pilot to ram her, but steam pressure had dropped so low we barely ran four knots. Gift clutched at a broken arm as Curtis sent the last shell slamming into the ironclad's bow. She turned away to avoid collision, and our starboard broadside guns raked her hull as we swept past with Vicksburg nearly in sight. We drifted by the last of the Federal ships and the shelling eased off. Only Read pounded away with his stern rifles as we sailed out of the volcano.

Steaming into the protective range of the Vicksburg batteries, the surviving crew crawled out of the hot, smoking casemate onto the decks and atop the shield. Their bodies were blackened and bloodied, their eyes wide in disbelief at the full miracle of our passage.

11

All of Vicksburg, it seemed, had turned out to watch the *Arkansas* meet her fate. Few of the spectators had expected to see us sail out of that cloud of smoke and round the bend above the city. Thousands of soldiers and townsfolk from every vantage point—behind guns, on front porches, from upstairs windows and rooftops—waved flags and handkerchiefs and cheered as we passed below the bluffs. We could hear their shouts from the deck.

It could hardly be called a victory, but after the loss of New Orleans and Memphis, the South took whatever good news it could get. And the numbers might have been worse: only ten men killed and fifteen seriously wounded on the *Arkansas*. But to most of us onboard, numbers mattered nothing. Hector cursed his friend Wallace for being "such a big dumb fool as to get killed," and then when told to "check that talk" began to sob like a child. Even worse, I learned that the same shell that had killed Thomas had torn across the gun deck and struck the bulwark above one of the stern gun crews just as Simon was bringing powder. He and two other men were killed. Out of the four Conroy brothers, only Peter remained alive—and he, too, had been badly wounded in the head.

Still, there were those who whooped and hollered when Midshipman Scales tied the stars and bars to a boat hook and wedged it into the grating atop the shield. Our colors had been shot away early on, along with both launch boats.

It was eight-fifty in the morning when the *Arkansas* tied up to the wharf at the foot of Jackson Street. A crowd of onlookers surged along the dockside as medical orderlies carried the dead and wounded ashore. Schoolboys not much younger than me gawked through the open ports at the wrecked and blood-soaked gun deck.

Jordi and I helped the orderlies pass Peter through one of the forward ports on a stretcher. He stared blankly, saying nothing. Of course I felt shocked and sad. But two words kept echoing in my brain like a bad song: *Not me! Not me!* Collins pulled an inch-long oak splinter out of my back, but apart from a few nicks and bruises I had no other injuries.

All the remaining Missouri artillery boys who were able gathered up their gear and filed off the boat to return to regular duty. Our crew was now halved in a stroke. Eagan gave us all of five minutes to get over the shock before barking clean-up orders. First we cleared the debris and then took hard brush brooms to the gun deck. The floor looked like that of a slaughterhouse, sticky with sand and blood, bits of hair and flesh in among the splintered wood. I pushed my broom, moving as if in a nightmare, trying not to be ill from the sweet, hot stench of it. I heard Albert shout in horror to Eagan when he found part of a blackened ear.

"But what do I do with it, sir?"

"Well, I doubt the poor son of a bitch wants it back."

And we all laughed like lunatics, apart from Albert, who wrapped it in a handkerchief and shoved it in his pocket like a newfound penny. The look on his face scared me. But still those words shouting in my head: *Not me! Not me!*

The sun rose hot in a clear blue sky, sparkling on the river. Just another summer morning, like yesterday, like every morning last week. Nothing different. But it all seemed somehow strange and new.

We filled buckets with river water and scrubbed the decks clean. Carpenters and machinists went to work on the damaged casemate. They worked fast, replacing the warped rail irons and the splintered timbers with grim efficiency.

A carriage arrived at the wharf with Generals Van Dorn and Breckinridge. They had watched the battle from the dome of the courthouse. Captain Brown wore a clean uniform with a fresh bandage under his cap. We stood to attention on the gun deck.

Van Dorn, a skinny, birdlike man, gave a nod. "Smart gunnery, gentlemen. Well fought."

That was all he had to say. Breckinridge spoke not at all. A tall man in a tailored uniform, with grand handlebar whiskers, he just peered into the gloom, looking hot and desperate to get back above deck. Climbing the main ladder way, he cracked his head on a beam. The crew struggled not to laugh.

Later that morning the *Arkansas* steamed down to the coal depot below town to refuel. None of the Federals had yet to harass us since we'd docked that morning under the Confederate guns. But as the crew got the coal chute into position, an armored side-wheel gunboat—the *Westfield*—steamed into range and opened on us with a 100-pound Parrott rifle. A few shots landed in the river close enough to spray the working party as the coal rumbled down the chute into our hold. But the only effect was to damp down the coal dust. We returned upriver to the wharf unpursued.

Just around noon one of the hotels in town sent down a wagon with lunch for the "brave crewmen of the *Arkansas*." We sat up under the deck awnings eating cured ham and potato salad and drinking fresh lemonade. It made a welcome break from cold, stale rations. Albert heaped his plate with food but then barely touched it. He just stared silently into the heat haze over the water. I wondered if the ear was still in his pocket.

Jordi lit his pipe. "Tell you what, I'll be glad when we sail down to the Gulf of Mexico. I'm sick of this damn river. I always wanted to go to sea."

Collins spat. "Are you really that dumb?"

Over the last two days Collins had drunk his supply of whisky and was now in a foul temper. "What do you mean by that?" Jordi snapped.

"We ain't gonna make it out of here," Collins replied. "Federals will be gunning for us soon enough. By nightfall, I wager."

"Let 'em come. We'll teach them another lesson," said Jordi. He had spent the entire battle on the lower deck bringing water to the firemen and engineers, and passing powder to the forward hatch.

"Like hell we will," said Collins. "This time they'll be prepared. So best say your prayers."

"Well, ain't you the optimist? Think you're better off drunk." Jordi took his plate away to the mess. Collins stared down at the shake in his hand and said nothing more.

But it was Albert who had me most worried. He seemed not to have heard a word spoken. I touched his elbow. "Are you okay?"

He didn't answer at first so I poked him hard in the ribs. He turned with a vacant look. I asked again.

"Never better," he said.

I lowered my voice. "What did you do with that ear?"

"I put it somewhere safe."

"Albert. That's crazy. What're you planning on doing with it?"

He stared back out over the water. "Work out who it belongs to."

"Are you serious?"

"Why not? It's just a simple matter of deduction, like a mathematics proof."

"And then what?"

"I'll send it to his family."

"Like in a parcel, through the post?" I hissed.

"Yes."

"Jesus, Albert. Imagine a mother opening that."

He raised his voice. "Don't you think she'd want it? If she loved her son?"

Collins said nothing, just shook his head sadly. I felt a sudden fury. "Just you stop acting crazy!" I shouted. "Throw it in the river."

"That would be the easy thing to do," he said. "Would you throw my ear in the river?"

An urge to punch him came over me. "I can't believe we're even talking about this," I replied. "Do whatever you want."

I stood up. The empty plate on my lap slid off and clattered down the side of the boat and into the river. Albert stared silently as it sank beneath the brown water. Just then Lieutenant Read called my name from the stern deck below and I turned away from my old friend without a second glance.

~

Just before sundown word came from observers upriver that enemy ships were raising steam—exactly as Collins had predicted. A long roll on the drum called us to our posts. All the repairs had been completed and the reserve gunners put in place. Gift had his arm in a sling and turned over command of his guns to Midshipman Scales.

Night fell black and moonless. Stevens ordered all the gun-port shutters closed to hide the glow of our lanterns. The casemate grew hot and airless and stank of unwashed men. We waited in silence for the next onslaught. But the panic I felt then was of a different sort. That afternoon I'd got the "trots" again and in the tension of the moment my bowels began to churn.

I heard a thundering roll of cannon and saw the glow of flares through the deck grating above us as the upper Confederate batteries opened fire on the Federal ships.

"Give 'em hell, boys," Eagan muttered from the hatchway and checked his watch.

Our guns were loaded and ready to run out. We just waited for the order from Stevens, who stood atop the shield with Gift and the captain. I clutched my belly, trying to hold on, but knew I had to go. "Sorry, sir," I whispered to Scales, who stood by the port Dahlgren. "I need the pot."

"Not now, Wood."

"Please, sir. I can't hold it."

He glared at me. "Go, then. But quickly."

"And don't fall in," said one of the regular sailors, and the crew laughed.

All the ports were shut so I snuck up the main ladder and climbed down the back shield to the stern deck. I hung my backside over the edge of the boat and emptied my bowels in the river. It was like some otherworldly hell out there. Above me on the dark bluff, countless cannons flashed with orange flame. The very air vibrated with the roar. Federal mortar shells fired from upriver glowed in high arcs like sky-rockets and fell into the unlit city with brilliant explosions. I sat with my back to the river, feeling greatly exposed.

Just as I reached for a rag in my pocket, a flash lit the sky and I glimpsed the line of darkened warships drifting downstream toward us. A huge three-masted sloop of war led the way, almost abreast now of our position at the wharf. Darkness and the rust color of our shield against the red clay bluffs hid us from the view of her gunners.

I heard Steven call down the hatch: "Mask lanterns and run out the guns."

I went to clean myself but the rag slipped from my hand into the river. Port tackle men heaved at their ropes and the heavy iron gun doors groaned open. Black cannon barrels slid out. I yanked up my trousers without caring and stumbled across the deck toward the steps up the back shield. A broadside thundered from the side of the *Arkansas*, knocking me off my feet. Shell fuses traced low over the dark river and struck the hull of the man-of-war with bright bursts of flame. I made it up the steps three at a time and leapt down the upper hatch as the man-of-war answered with a cannon salvo.

A shell splintered into our hull inches above the waterline. The *Arkansas* shuddered sickly. A blast of hot air and smoke blew up from the lower hatch.

Stevens pushed me out the way and hollered below. "Report!"

A voice below coughed and answered. "Took it through the engine room, sir. Gillmore's dead. Dispensary's wrecked."

"Secure a hose and get that fire out." Stevens slid down the ladder into the smoky gloom.

"Position! God rot you," Eagan snarled low as I passed, his scar bone white.

~

Scales had the port guns run out again in minutes and poured another broadside into the next passing ship. All hint of the sullen schoolboy was gone. He bellowed orders and curses at his crewman, the drill now almost like a dance: Wet sponges hissing down hot barrels, powder and shot and rag driven tight with plungers. The screech of tackle and carriage wheels as the guns ran forward, the shout of "Ready, Fire!" Hands over ears, men jerking the lanyards, and finally, the blast.

Back and forth I dashed with my pass box, feeding powder to the guns, my stomach cramps forgotten.

No one on the gun deck bothered counting the number of ships that steamed past us that night, pouring salvo after salvo into our position below the bluff. It seemed endless, absurd, the amount of firepower directed against one small boat. I had just taken another powder bag from Eagan when the firing suddenly stopped. A blessed silence fell; nothing apart from the ringing in my ears and the distant rumble-on of the lower batteries.

Only a single man had fallen on the gun deck—Ab Gardner, one of the medical orderlies. A fragment of shot had ricocheted through an open port and struck him in the temple. He was only eighteen.

Lieutenant Barbot's dog Nick had somehow managed to slip his rope during the bombardment. No one had noticed until the shooting ended how the little dog was dancing around Gardner's corpse, licking the blood that spilled out of his head. Midshipman Scales went into a fury and kicked the dog clear across the deck. It struck the bulkhead with a sharp yelp and scurried down the hatch.

Barbot saw this and wordlessly pulled a cutlass from his belt. Eagan tackled him as he charged for Scales. Read wrenched the sword from Barbot's hand.

"You're a dead man," Barbot shouted at Scales. "I demand satisfaction!"

Just then Captain Brown appeared down the main ladder way. "The only satisfaction either of you'll get is a court-martial if a single drop of blood is shed among my crew," he growled. "We've an entire enemy fleet happy to oblige us of that. Mr. Eagan, I want both officers confined to quarters. Get poor Gardner below."

Two other men had been killed in the bombardment. An 11-inch shot had knocked both engines off their mountings and destroyed the ship's medical supplies before imbedding in the bulwark opposite. That long day ended with more bodies and wounded men to be lifted ashore, and more work for the ship's carpenters and engineers.

~

Next morning I awoke at sunrise among a mass of sleeping men atop the shield. Only the officers seemed willing to bear the heat in their staterooms below deck. I threaded my way among the bedrolls and hammocks and down to the stern. I took a leak and then dropped a bucket in the river upstream to get some water for a wash. All was quiet and a thin mist lay over the river. Hoisting up the bucket, I heard a deep *boom* upriver. Maybe a second later another report answered from the river below. Two smoking fuse trails rose into the blue sky, one to the south, one to the north. My only thought then was that it seemed a bit early for the Federals to start their daily bombardment of the Confederate emplacements up the bluff.

I pulled the bucket onto the deck and soaked my neckerchief to scrub my face. Looking up again, I saw the smoke trails now arcing high overhead on convergent paths like symmetric curves in a geometry problem. Just for a moment the missiles seemed to hang in the air above me and then began to fall with a shrill whistle, aimed (or so it seemed) square between my eyes. I jumped to my feet and knocked the bucket back into the river.

THE PASSAGE

I scrambled up the steps to the upper deck and hollered, "Look out! It's us they're bombing!"

Heads rose from bedrolls. A few men struggled to their feet and leapt off the shield toward the muddy bank. Others just watched in horror as the shells screamed down upon us. The first hit the river and exploded about fifty yards off the stern with a giant fountain of water. The second fell no closer, off the port, only spraying us with a fine mist.

Brown rushed up onto deck with the other officers. All the men still in their bedrolls laughed at those now climbing up the bank, covered in mud. A few cursed at me but one of the regular seamen shouted, "Come on now, fellers. Wood just meant to wake us in case we missed out the pleasure of a horrible death." The crew laughed, even the officers. I blushed bright red.

All that day and over the next week, Federal gun crews upriver and down ranged on us with their mortars, Farragut's strategy being not to risk another direct attack. To hit a city from a range of two and a half miles is one thing, to hit a small boat is another. A couple of shells did fall close enough to pepper the decks with iron fragments, but mostly it was just unnerving.

~

Temperatures that first day and the next at Vicksburg reached one hundred degrees. The iron casing on the boat grew hot enough to fry an egg. Soon the hea began to take a serious toll on the crew. Each morning the sick list grew longer with dysentery and malarial fevers. Surgeon Hix kept us dosed with quinine but to little avail. Even he came down with the fever and had to be taken off the boat to the Marine Hospital.

The second night Jordi took a chill. He sat on deck wrapped in a blanket, shivering, though the air temperature was hardly below eighty-five. By morning he looked deathly gray. I brought him water, but his hand shook such that I had to hold the cup up to his mouth. I touched his forehead. It burned with fever.

"Think you may be in line for a short vacation."

"Or a shallow grave," he said, teeth chattering.

"Not a chance. Think you passed through the valley of death just to pop off like a fly to a little fever?"

Jordi grinned and then reached under his blanket. He brought out two items. "Could you give these to the payroll clerk for safekeeping? Don't want no Johnny Reb stealing 'em while I don't know better."

One of the items was the sketch that Liz had given him, the other a gold and enamel cameo locket on a fine gold chain. "You can have a look if you like," he said.

I opened the locket. Inside was a miniature portrait of a young woman with long curly brown hair, dark eyes, and pale skin, a rose flush high on her cheeks. I could see the resemblance.

"That's my mother," said Jordi. "My father had that painted in the French Quarter before I was born."

"She was beautiful."

"Yeah. Just not beautiful enough for him to make her respectable. You know, I used to see him sometimes. He took coffee at Masperos on Chartres Street. I'm not sure he even knew I existed. Just another one of his bastards. But at least she got that off him."

I closed the locket and slipped it into my trouser pocket. "I'll make sure they're safe."

"Thanks," he said and grasped my arm.

That afternoon an ambulance took him up the hill with the other sick crewmen. I worried it might be the last I'd see of Jordi Autin.

~

Our crew had now been diminished to less than a quarter its original number. Brown asked Van Dorn for more men, but the commander agreed only to issue a general call for volunteers among the forces now encamped at Vicksburg. A few turned up at the wharf, but the sight of the shot-battered iron shield turned most away.

With Surgeon Hix now out of action, Captain Brown also telegraphed Jackson for medical volunteers. A day or so later a doctor, a tall, serious-looking young man with owl-like spectacles, arrived from Clinton. His name was Taft, and he came so well recommended that the captain gave him an on-the-spot appointment as acting ship's surgeon. He had arrived early, before the Federals began their daily pastime of shelling us. Stevens took him on a tour of the boat, which looked perfectly shipshape—the shield armor repaired, decks scrubbed, awnings spread. The doctor then had breakfast in the wardroom. He seemed to find his duties somewhat of a lark.

"Your iron shield seems virtually impregnable," I heard him comment blandly. "Just what is there for a ship's surgeon to do?"

Only later, when shown the splintered path made by the 11-inch shell crashing through the dispensary, did he appear a little less confident. And then the Federal mortars got going. Come lunchtime, Surgeon Taft could be found hugging the companion ladder, white-faced and rattled. Each time a shell screamed into the river and exploded, he'd moan, "Oh! Louisa and the babes."

One early morning Gift took me aside for a word. We stood on the bow looking upriver toward Tuscumbia Bend. His broken arm was still strapped in a sling. Half his beard had been singed away and the skin underneath was crusted and peeling. He got straight to the point.

"Stevens has decided to promote you to ordinary seaman. You report to McCalla. You'll be working the forward port Columbiad. Do well and Captain Brown will see about getting you a commission from Richmond."

I was more pleased than I ever expected. I asked without thinking, "And Albert, sir?"

I assumed with the shortage of men the same logic would apply. Gift looked annoyed.

"Just worry about doing your own job."

"Yes sir," I said. "And thank you."

"Congratulations," he replied and climbed back up the shield.

~

McCalla reckoned I was too slight to be a side-tackle man, so he made me the sponger on his gun crew. My job was to swab out the cannon barrel using a wet woolen sponge attached to the end of a wooden staff. This had to be done after each firing; otherwise a spark from the unextinguished gunpowder residue could ignite the next cartridge, causing it to explode in the barrel.

"Ain't just housekeeping," said McCalla. "I seen a dirty gun take out a sponger and a loader."

Two days I drilled with McCalla's crew until we had the firing sequence down like clockwork. This meant being excused from most of my old duties. One afternoon McCalla let us outside the forward gun port for a breather and a sip of water. I noticed Albert and Collins up the riverbank along with a couple of other men, digging a latrine trench under a mercilessly hot sun.

Morgan, another Texas seaman who worked as loader on the crew, followed my gaze. "Suppose things could be worse," he snorted. "Poor devils."

I had been avoiding Albert since our run-in that first day at Vicksburg. I now spent most of the time with my new gun crew. Albert seemed to have retreated into a world of his own. Collins came to me one night and said that Albert had begun to talk aloud to himself on work detail. Other men would tell him to shut up but it made no difference.

"What can I do?" I replied, the words again in my head: *Not me. Not me.*

"Talk to him. You're his best friend."

I shrugged. "I've tried to."

"How hard?" he asked.

To be truthful, I had begun to find Albert more an embarrassment than a friend. We were in a different world now, among men of action. Albert was just not up to it. I didn't want to be tainted with his oddness, his failure.

Collins went to Taft and then to Captain Brown to ask that Albert be discharged and sent home. But Brown said that the *Arkansas* needed all the men she could get, no matter how crazy.

That night after evening mess I found Albert up on deck, already lying on his bedroll. The daily shelling had stopped. A red sky fringed the horizon. Few of the other men were about. I crouched down next to him.

"Looks like the Federals have laid off early tonight," I said. "Must be the admiral's birthday or something."

Albert lay unmoving.

I continued: "McCalla thinks we might have some action tomorrow—"

"I'd love to discuss naval matters with you, Sam," he interrupted, "but I'm just too damn tired."

"Sorry," I said, but again my temper got the best of me. "Suppose you want me to apologize for getting a promotion, for taking my job seriously."

Albert didn't reply.

I stood up. "Maybe if you showed yourself just a little more willing."

"Thank you, sir. I'll try harder," he muttered and rolled over onto his side.

I wanted to kick him. "There's just no point talking to you anymore," I said.

Again I got no reply.

~

Later, before turning in, I sat up under one of the running lights and pulled out Nancy's letter. The paper had grown frayed being in and out of my pocket so much. It was stained with blood and sweat. Her lace handkerchief was long gone, still with Wallace, wherever that was. I read her words once again, seeking only those that spoke to me: friendship, fondly, tears, love. All the others—bravery, sacrifice, courage, nation—seemed drained of meaning from constant repetition. Nothing more than scratches on paper.

12

I awoke in darkness to the long roll of Hollins's drum. Observers upriver had reported activity among the Federal fleet. I yanked on my boots and trousers and stowed away my bedroll. Lanterns burned bright inside the gun deck. I filled my swab bucket from the river and took my position by the gun port.

Stevens arrived for inspection and looked about the deck in disbelief. "Is this all of us?"

"Yes sir," Eagan replied.

Only twenty-eight crewmen and officers remained out of more than two hundred that had sailed from Yazoo City just a week before. We had gunners enough for only two full crews. Mine would have to double on the stern rifles should the need arise. Brown came below and spoke by the forward guns.

"Gentlemen. Word from the upper batteries is that Federal ironclads are underway and we can expect an attack shortly. I'll say only this: the day-to-day survival of this vessel serves as a direct affront to the might of the Federal Navy. The fight can only get more brutal. This crew—be it sorely diminished—has proven itself equal under the worst odds. I know you can do so again."

Eagan then shouted, "Three cheers for the captain!"

And we answered, "Hurrah, hurrah, hurrah!"

One of the new volunteers, a boy named Tredwell, looked suddenly gray and vomited onto the deck. Eagan cursed the boy and made him mop up the mess. I laughed along with the rest of the veterans. That morning I felt oddly calm, almost jubilant at the prospect of another fight, "battle happy" as Read called it. Twice I had survived major attacks with hardly a scratch. I felt indestructible.

I saw Albert across the deck, standing with his pass box by the rear hatch. I grinned and shouted, "You ready?"

He stared back as if I were a stranger.

A few seconds later we heard the Confederate river batteries open fire. Below deck the only two remaining firemen heaved coal into the furnaces to raise steam in the boilers, in case we needed to run out from shore and engage the enemy. From my position by the barrel of the forward Columbiad I could see upriver. Emerging from the smoke of the upper cannonade came three Federal ironclads churning downriver in a line. First was the *Essex*, a big blunt-nosed gunboat that looked like a barge fitted with a tall iron box. Smoke poured from her twin stacks as she steamed at full power with the current, aimed direct for our bow.

"Think she means to ram us!" Stevens shouted.

Brown ordered a deckhand to ease up on the forward hawser that tied us to the wharf. He then shouted at the engineer to give a touch to the starboard propeller. Our bow swung out into the current to allow our forward guns to range on the *Essex*, which was bearing down upon us. Lieutenant Gift shouted "Fire when ready!" and I jumped clear of the loaded Columbiad.

McCalla yanked the lanyard and the cannon roared. The shell rang off the front of the Federal without piercing her armor. Midshipman Scales fired the second Columbiad, but to no further effect. I ran to my position and plunged my sponge staff hissing into the hot barrel. Morgan then loaded a cartridge bag followed by another heavy 8-inch shell and wadding. He pushed in his plunger and rammed it tightly home. Heave men yanked the tackle ropes to run the gun back out.

Just then the *Essex* eased up on her engines to avoid impaling herself on our sharp iron prow. Our Columbiads fired again but the shells could not pierce her thick armor. The river current pushed the Federal out of the forward line of fire. Lieutenant Stevens shouted for crews to man the broadside cannons. Just before I left the forward port I glimpsed the big ironclad out in the river about fifty yards off, her iron gun shutters groaning open, black barrels running out, ready to fire.

I took up position beside the forward larboard gun

and gripped my sponge staff, waiting for Stevens to order the first broadside. My thoughts focused only on the big Dahlgren cannon, moving in after the blast recoil, ready to swab out the barrel for the next shot.

Stevens shouted to the crew, "Get ready to repel any boarders!"

I turned back to the gun. Morgan reached down to the cutlass in his belt. Gift peered low through the gun ports, waiting for the *Essex* to drift in line.

I remember little of what happened next: a loud roar as the *Essex* fired her bow guns; the shudder as the solid shot hit; a blast of hot air, wood, and iron splinters whistling through the air. I came to again maybe a second or so later, lying on the deck covered in blood. I couldn't even be certain that it was my own. All around me lay dead and wounded men. I felt no pain, just shock, but knew better than to look down at my leg. I tasted blood in my mouth, felt broken teeth. My tongue probed a hole in my cheek.

Looking up, I saw Albert leaning over me. He was shouting. But I could hear nothing, just a loud roaring in my ears.

"Orderly, orderly!" he seemed to mouth, and then, taking my hand, he said something else I couldn't make out. A second later another explosion rocked the boat. Smoke and debris blasted over me. I opened my eyes again and Albert was gone.

All was confusion, men running with fire buckets and stretchers. Someone kicked me hard in passing. I screamed Albert's name but couldn't hear the sound of my own voice. Turning my head again, I then found him lying on his back a few feet away. Blood pooled out from under his head. He lay there opening and closing his mouth like a fish out of water. I screamed his name again but then all went black.

~

I awoke below deck atop a table in the temporary surgery. Bixby held one of my arms. He looked gray and shaken. I heard him say, "Wait. He's conscious."

Surgeon Taft peered down at me, eyes wide, spectacles spattered with blood. I tried to speak, to ask about Albert, but a bandage had been tied around my cheek and under my chin.

"Just take it easy, Wood," Bixby said gently.

"Chloroform!" shouted Taft.

Someone placed an acrid smelling lint bandage over my mouth. I looked up again at Bixby. He gripped my arm tightly and tried to smile. A moment later I was out again.

Bright sunlight and the tickle of flies brushing my face woke me. I opened my eyes to a brilliant blue sky. I lay in an ambulance wagon with another man unmoving on the next pallet. A sharp pain burned in my lower right leg. I reached down to rub it but felt nothing there. I sat up and saw the bandaged stump just below my knee. I started screaming. Two medical orderlies jumped in the wagon and held me by the arms. One of them put a hand over my mouth. I passed out and woke again as the wagon trundled along the road. Each rut thumped my head against the hard wagon bed but I didn't care. I just stared up into the blue and wept.

The ambulance took us up to Marine Hospital, a three-story brick building just a few blocks downriver. Orderlies moved me onto a cot bed in a long, narrow ward on the third floor. It was filled with dozens of sick and wounded men from the *Arkansas* and other army units. The place smelled of urine and rotting meat.

I remember little of that day. I just lay there in shock, numbed and unthinking. A sparrow fluttered among the rafters, too frightened to fly down and out an open window. All day I watched it beat against the skylight and flit from one end of the ceiling to the other.

I must have been weakened from loss of blood, for that evening I took a chill. I fell in and out of sleep, plagued by fevered dreams, melding each into another. In one I had returned home and was walking up the track to Sandhill with the clouds low and threatening. Nothing remained of Grandfather's house but a ruin. All our possessions lay scattered across the yard, burnt and broken. I ran to the burial ground among the cedars and found Liz standing before a fresh grave. "Did you have fun playing soldier?" she asked. And when I asked whose grave it was, she replied, "Guess," and clapped her hands with a grin. "A guessing game. It'll be fun." I told her not to be a fool, to tell me. But she just kept saying, "Come on. Guess." And the dream faded.

In another I walked with Nancy under a bright moon in the woods along the river. She kissed me and let go of my hand and ran laughing down the trail without looking back. I chased after her, running faster and faster, but couldn't catch up. The trail began to narrow. The woods ahead grew choked with vines and briars. Nancy just seemed to vanish into the thicket. But I could still hear her laughing. Briars tore at my clothes, the forest grew darker and darker. Then I awoke, only to fall into another dream and another, in endless succession.

Morning came. Bright sunlight streamed through the skylight. My head felt as if it were caught in a clamp. I opened my eyes and there by my bed stood Albert. He wore his cap and naval jacket. His shirt-front was still stained with blood.

"I thought you were dead," I said weakly.

He grinned. "Must not be if I'm here talking to you."

He took off his cap and looked about the ward, the bustle of doctors and orderlies, the groaning and whispered talk of the patients. "Charming place."

"Yeah, ain't it," I replied.

He looked down at my cot. "Sorry about your leg. Could be worse."

I found that an odd thing for Albert to say, a cruel edge to it. "How could it be any worse?" I snapped.

He smiled. "Well, you could be dead."

"Thanks. I'll hold on to that."

"What was it you were gonna do?" he asked. "Fly around my bed playing your harp?"

"Yeah," I said. "And you were gonna swat me with your Bible."

We both laughed. Albert looked a gray shade of pale. His eyes were hollow from lack of rest.

"Jesus. You're a mess," I said. "Why not go back to the boat? Get some sleep. Change your uniform."

Albert looked down at his stained shirt. He reached up and touched the cloth, pulling away bloody fingertips. He looked up at me in horror.

"You're bleeding," I said.

I tried to sit up to shout for an orderly but the pain in my head knocked me back flat. I closed my eyes and hollered, "Could someone help my friend here!"

And then quieter to Albert: "Stay put now. A doctor'll come soon enough."

But when I opened my eyes again, he'd gone. I sat up and searched the ward franticallly. A gray-bearded soldier lay propped on the bed next to me reading a newspaper.

"Where did my friend go?" I asked him.

He looked annoyed. "You're dreaming, son. And I tell you what, we'd all appreciate you doing it a bit quieter."

~

My fever raged for days. I could hardly tell what was real from what was phantom. No one seemed to pay me much mind except to bring sips of water and wash my brow. One night I awoke with the ward in darkness. A figure moved between the beds, a girl all in black, with dark hair and eyes, pale skin. She held a candle and, seeing me awake, seemed to glide to my bedside. She reached down to touch my forehead.

"Are you the angel of death?" I asked in dread.

She smiled and whispered, "Hardly. Go on back to sleep now."

Next morning I awoke and my fever had broken. One of the orderlies brought me a glass of water.

"Thank you," I croaked. My cheek was sore from the stitching and my tongue rasped on the two broken teeth.

"Good to be back in the land of the living?" he asked and laid a soft hand on my shoulder. "You had us all worried."

His name was Eli, a small boyish-looking man of about twenty, with a round, friendly face and long brown hair.

"How about some breakfast?"

"I'm not hungry."

"Come on now. You've not eaten for days," said Eli.

"Days?" I asked.

"Three days, at least. So you need to get something down. Build your strength."

I sat up and asked him about Albert. Over in the next bed the gray-bearded soldier, a man called Talbot, gave a stage cough.

"Only visitor I know of was an officer by the name of Read," Eli answered. "He came yesterday while you were sleeping. So what will it be? How about some honey grits to start? Easy on the stomach."

Talbot lowered his newspaper. "Watch he don't push none of his quacker food on you."

"Hush," said Eli. "He means Quaker. I'm a Quaker from up near Corinth."

"That's what I said, quacker."

"The soul of wit is our Talbot here," replied Eli.

He brought me a bowl of hominy grits drizzled with honey. The first bite rekindled my hunger and I ate the entire bowl. This seemed to genuinely please Eli.

"Last night I saw a girl in black," I asked him in a low voice. "Was she real? I don't know what's real anymore."

Eli chuckled. "She's real enough. That'd be Lydia. Doctor Hilliard's daughter."

Eli brought porridge and weak milk coffee. Breakfast made me feel tired again, and I drowsed for an hour or so. Opening my eyes, I found the girl in black again at my bedside, looking not nearly so spectral in the morning light. I sat up with a start.

"Don't worry. I won't touch you again," she said.

"Sorry about that," I said. "What I called you."

"It's okay. I've been called worse."

She looked about fifteen or sixteen, with a thin face, not beautiful like Nancy's but striking. Her large dark eyes were full of spark.

"I'm Lydia. My father runs the ward here. He's the surgeon."

Her handshake was surprisingly firm. She then reached into a pocket on the front of her dress.

"One of the orderlies found this with your clothes," she pulled out Nancy's letter. "I didn't read it. That is, I didn't mean to read it."

She looked shamefaced and handed me the letter.

"Is she your sweetheart?" she asked, but immediately seemed to regret her words. "Sorry. That's none of my business."

"It's okay," I said. "She was, I think. I can't be sure now."

"Why?"

"Well, who'd want a beau with a missing leg?"

Lydia looked suddenly serious, almost annoyed. "Well, if she loves you it won't matter. Will it?"

But again she wrung her hands and blushed. I slipped the note under my pillow. Lydia hesitated and then took a deep breath.

"She writes a good letter though. Very..." She paused to weigh her words. "Very ennobling. Well... in any case, there it is. Returned. Glad you're feeling better."

And she swung quickly on her heel and marched away.

Talbot chuckled to himself behind his newspaper.

∼

Later that afternoon Read came to visit again. He wore his full dress uniform, sword and scabbard at his side, gold epaulettes on his shoulders. Walking across the ward, he raised a handkerchief up to his nose. I'd long grown accustomed to the stench. Upon seeing me, he slipped it back into his pocket.

"Wood. Looking better."

He shook my hand and glanced about, saying loudly, "I do hate hospitals. Just end up making you more sick. You get out of here quick as you can."

He gazed down at my cot.

"Damned sorry about your leg. Puts paid to a naval career and all. But am I right, Wood, in thinking you weren't exactly sold on the idea anyway?"

"No sir," I replied. "I guess not."

"Well, I'm sure you'll do fine in whatever endeavor you choose. You're a smart one."

He then dropped a bundle of cigars on my blanket. "Brought you these," he said. "Smoking can be a great comfort."

I thanked him, and then asked the question I'd been dreading to have answered. "Could you tell me where my friend Albert is?"

Read spoke matter-of-factly: "Well, I suppose they took him on up to the churchyard for burial. But I did also hear the town was clearing another plot for military graves…"

He then noticed the look on my face. "You did know he was dead?"

"I-I wasn't certain."

"Sorry. I just assumed…"

I felt my eyes my water up. Read turned away.

"Good man, Ledbetter, if kind of strange. Keeping that ear and all. Eagan found it among his things, in an envelope along with a sheet of paper with all the names of the dead, lots of lines and squiggles. He'd worked out it belonged to one of the Missouri boys—Grady. Brown had it sent up to the minister…"

But I can't say I was listening. I'd known the truth all along; I just couldn't face it.

Read rocked on his heels uncomfortably. His face then brightened. "Did anyone see fit to tell you that Farragut upped anchor yesterday and sailed away downriver?"

"The fleet's gone?" I asked.

"Don't that just beat all? Captain reckons it finally dawned on him that no naval force could reduce Vicksburg. Need an army to do that. We got the *Arkansas* now under full repair, just waiting for orders. So you keep us in your prayers."

Read reached into his satchel. "Also brought you this."

He flourished my copy of Tennyson. "Half a league, half a league, half a league onward…." He placed it next to the cigars.

"I'll get Eagan to send up the rest of your gear, along with Ledbetter's since you two were close. Got to go now. Van Dorn has invited every officer in town to a congratulatory ball. Hence the fancy duds."

Read bent down to shake my hand again. "Okay, Wood. You take care now."

He then put on his cap and hurried away out the front entrance. I found it surprising, my sadness at watching him go. Maybe it was just because now there was no reason to ever see Charles W. Read again.

After dinner I asked Eli for a pen, paper, and some ink. I wrote two letters: one to the family and one to Nancy. I couldn't bring myself to write to Albert's parents. Not then.

It was odd. Somehow just putting the words on paper, imagining their effect, seemed to confirm all that had happened was real—my leg, Albert's death. Like drawing up a formal contract, exchanging past for present. Both letters were short and brutal, empty of hope. No wonder Nancy never wrote back.

~

Next morning the grim truth began to sink in. I was a cripple. Long before dawn I lay awake, making a list in my head. Never again would I run or dance or climb a tree or bound up the stairs. No more long hunts up on the ridge, no more dragging the skiff down to the river for fishing, no chasing Sloeberry around the pasture to saddle her for a ride. On and on went my list. This was how I tortured myself for what had happened to Albert, for what I'd done. For the things I'd said to him in the last weeks, the things I'd not said. This was my punishment.

Men began to stir on the ward. Eli came later with morning coffee and porridge on a tin tray. I told him to leave it on the box crate that served as my bedside table.

"Okay. But sit up and eat before it gets cold."

I rolled into my blanket and closed my eyes. I did not want to eat, did not feel I deserved to eat. Only sleep appealed and even that wouldn't come. Eli returned ten minutes later and poked me in back. "Sit up, you."

"Not hungry." I said.

He poked me again, hard. "No matter. You sit up and eat. I'll feed you like a baby if necessary."

Talbot commented from his bed: "Thought you quackers were nonviolent. Stop prodding the boy. Says he ain't hungry."

But Eli pulled my blanket off. "Eat that porridge! It's cold now but that's your own damn fault."

I sat up. He put the tray in my lap and stood there, arms folded, while I ate the entire bowl and drank my coffee.

~

Talbot proved to be a talker. That morning I got his life story. Told me how he belonged to an artillery regiment from Louisiana. Both his sons had gone off to fight in Virginia, and he couldn't stand the quiet in the house. So he left his wife in tears and went off to Baton Rouge to enlist.

A week ago he'd fallen from a wagon and badly broken his leg. Doctor Hilliard told him he'd be no use to the army anymore, but Talbot vowed not to return home as long as his sons were still in the firing line.

All day long I listened without comment to his stories, his opinions, his gripes. Not that he seemed to notice my silence. And it did take my mind off things.

Later that afternoon Lydia came to visit again. She wore the same black dress. In her hand was a white rose.

"Thought you might like to see something from the world outside," she said and handed me the blossom. "They come up like weeds all around the hospital."

Talbot grinned. "Don't I get one?"

Lydia seemed used to his banter. "It can be for you and Mr. Wood to share."

He chuckled and raised his newspaper.

Lydia sat down on the end of my cot. "Eli says he's going to get you up on crutches soon. Then you can go for a walk around the grounds."

"Go for a *walk?*"

Lydia grew flustered. "Just to get some fresh air."

I immediately felt sorry for the remark. She then noticed the Tennyson sitting on the crate by my cot. She reached over to pick it up. "Will I read to you? I read to some of the other patients."

Lydia opened the book to the contents page. "What'll it be, 'The Charge of the Light Brigade'?"

"No, thank you. I've heard enough of that one."

She raised an eyebrow. "Sorry. And I came to cheer you up." She closed the book and gave it back to me. "Tomorrow I'll bring something a little lighter."

~

That next afternoon and the next, Lydia came to visit. I began to mark the passing of each day with her arrival. One morning Eli brought a pair of crutches and helped me to stand. The rush of blood to my stump seared like a hot knife. But I managed to make it out to a bench on a small balcony overlooking the Mississippi. I sat there soaked in sweat with my efforts, watching the boats ply the river again with the Federals now gone. Just ten days ago, all that fire and smoke, fighting and death, and now it seemed as if life was back to normal. I couldn't help but wonder if it had all been pointless, if everything was pointless.

Eli came out later with his mid-morning coffee and sat next to me. I asked him why Lydia always wore black.

"She lost her brother this past April," he said. "He was killed at Shiloh. His name was Gibb. Lydia's not worn anything but black since that day."

He dumped his coffee into a flowerpot and sighed, "Place of peace."

"Pardon?" I said.

"Shiloh is Hebrew for 'place of peace.' There's a Quaker community near where the battle took place. My Uncle Benjamin's family lives up there. You do know that Quakers believe war is a sin? That's why I work here. I refuse to fight. But I had to do something. How can anyone sit back and do nothing with such terrible things going on?"

Eli rose to go back inside.

"But let me tell you—Lydia out-Quakers the Quakers. She hates this war, just about as much as she loved her brother. Seeing all these sick and broken soldiers just makes it worse. Opinions like that don't go down well among the gaggle in town. Not that she seems to care much."

~

My other regular visitor was Doctor Hilliard. He came by every morning on his rounds, a tall white-haired man, always clean shaven with a high stiff collar and a deep sonorous voice. I could see the likeness to Lydia in his eyes. Every few days he'd remove the bandages on my stump and sniff for any hint of gangrene in the wound.

"No finer diagnostic instrument could a doctor possess," he'd say, tapping his nose. "Apart maybe from the eyes."

He'd then declare my wound to be healing well. One morning he pulled out a pair of scissors and snipped away the sutures in my cheek. He brushed a finger over the raised skin.

"Make a fine dueling scar, that. Something to tell your grandchildren about."

He then sat on the end of my cot. "Lydia tells me you're from Yazoo City. That's not too far up the road. It's about time we began thinking about getting you home. I'd like you to start taking a little more exercise out around the grounds. Build your strength back up. Then we can arrange some suitable transport back to Yazoo City. No point staying here any longer than necessary."

Much as the hospital was uncomfortable—hot, airless, devoid of any privacy—I began to dread the prospect of going home, of being surrounded by painful reminders, of having to answer all the questions, to account for all the details. I yearned to see Grandfather and Martha and Liz again. But so much now in my soul was different, stripped away, old assumptions turned inside out. How could I hope to reoccupy my old life?

War had not made a man of me. It had only killed the boy I was.

13

One Sunday afternoon about two weeks into my hospital stay Lydia lent me her copy of *The Pickwick Papers*, and I sat reading out under a shade tree on the hospital grounds. A wagon turned into the entrance and began to trudge up the hill. To my surprise, seated beside the driver was Jordi, looking fully recovered from his fever. I shouted, and he leapt off the wagon and ran across the lawn. His eye lingered only a moment on my crutches and the empty trouser leg as he dropped onto the grass next to me, out of breath.

"Eagan sent over your things," he said. "Gave me an hour's leave to come along with the driver. The *Arkansas* departs tomorrow."

"For where?"

"Baton Rouge," he replied. "It's a total fiasco."

Jordi told me how Van Dorn had ordered the *Arkansas* to steam downriver and provide gun support for an attack to take back Baton Rouge from the

Federals. General Breckinridge had already left by rail with five thousand men.

"They're sending the *Arkansas* without her repairs being finished," Jordi said. "And Captain Brown isn't back yet. He took ill while on leave visiting his family over in Grenada County. Lieutenant Stevens is in charge."

Worst of all, he added, the chief engineer from the *Arkansas* lay in a hotel room up in town, suffering with exhaustion and high fever. Only his skill had kept the boat's two temperamental engines functioning on the trip down to Vicksburg.

"Stevens keeps getting telegrams from the captain telling him not to move until he returns," said Jordi. "But Van Dorn insists we're to cast off before first light. I don't think the general will be happy 'til we're all dead, or worse."

He glanced at my leg and then muttered, "Sorry. I didn't mean...."

"It's okay," I said. "So what do you think of the tailoring? Kind of long in the cuff."

He shook his head. "And there I was, lying up in a hospital bed."

"Glad to see you better," I said. "You had me and Collins worried."

"Think the fever was worrying? You should've seen my nurse."

"Was she nice?"

"About two hundred fifty pounds and called Bobby," he replied, and we both laughed.

Jordi told me other news from the boat. Bixby had gotten drunk again after the last attack and ended up AWOL in the Vicksburg jail. Lieutenant Gift had only just yesterday got him released. Collins had sworn off the whiskey and been promoted to gunner's mate. Most surprising of all, though, Peter Conroy had recovered from his wound and returned for duty.

"Stevens wanted to send him home," Jordi explained. "Said that losing three sons was heartache enough for one family. But Peter told him that if they put him off the boat, he'd just walk straight to the first enlistment office and join the infantry. So Stevens let him stay. Peter's working your old crew. It's good to have old faces among all them new recruits."

Just then Lydia appeared out on the porch of the surgeon's quarters and walked across the grass toward us.

Jordi sat up for a better view. "Things don't look so bad here to me."

I made introductions. Jordi held her hand and did his "Autins of New Orleans" routine, but Lydia looked unconvinced. She invited us up to the house and we drank lemonade until the driver hollered for Jordi.

I followed him down to the wagon. Climbing back on the buckboard Jordi reached into his coat pocket for a letter. He held it out to me with a shy grin.

"Could you give this to Liz when you get home? Hope all the spelling's okay. Collins helped me write it."

"She'll be pleased to hear from you," I said. "Come visit us at Sandhill first chance you get."

Jordi shook my hand. "Thank you. I will."

The wagon pulled away and trundled back down the drive. Jordi stood and waved as it pulled out the gate. My heart ached to watch him go. I seemed to have so few friends left.

Eagan had sent Albert's possessions and mine packed in a sea chest: civilian clothes, shoes, spare uniforms, books, money. It was all there, far as I could tell. I opened Albert's copy of *Principles and Practice in Integral Calculus*. An envelope fell out. It was addressed, "To my parents in the event of my death," and was sealed and dated 20 July—two days before he died. Had he had some premonition? I couldn't help but wonder what he'd written about me. Had he told them what kind of friend I'd turned out to be in the end? I opened the book to replace the envelope and saw that a label printed with the crest of Yazoo Academy had been pasted to the inside cover. On it Mr. Anders had written "Top Student, Mathematics, 1860" and this inscription:

> *Beauty in things exists in the mind*
> *which contemplates them.*
> —DAVID HUME

~

That night I slept restlessly. Some time in the dark hours of morning I awoke and got out of bed with my crutches to get some air on the balcony. A quarter moon hung low in the sky. Looking out over the river, I caught sight of the *Arkansas*. She'd cast off her lines and turned into the current downriver. Orange lantern light glowed from her hatches and open gun ports. Bright sparks swirled amid the black smoke rising from her single stack. On she went down toward the bend, shadowy figures moving about her deck, unknowing, indifferent to my watching.

~

That next afternoon I sat with Lydia as she scraped linen sheets to make lint for bandages. A thunderstorm boiled over the lowlands across the river in Louisiana, bringing a cooling breeze.

"I like your friend, Jordi," she said. "He reminds me of my brother."

"How's that?" I asked.

"Just always teasing. Gibb was like that. I remember when I was little and would get angry at Father. I'd sometimes announce that I was running away from home. Gibb would follow me to my room and help me pack. He'd say: 'Maybe you should take an extra petticoat just in case.' Then he'd wave me off at the gate. 'Don't forget to write.' I never got beyond the next field before running home. He'd still be at the gate. 'Back so soon?' he'd say. 'Sorry. We already sold your toys.' It didn't get any better as he grew up. Never dull with Gibb around."

I told her about Jordi's childhood and she shook her head.

"It's a wonder how some people manage to take one step after another." She reached out to take my hand. "We're all being tested now."

Across the river the big storm rolled southward. I clutched her hand, small and cool, in mine and felt something most unlikely given my circumstances: hope.

~

Two days later word came that the *Arkansas* had been sunk just above Baton Rouge. Details slowly began to filter in. That early morning after I watched her leave Vicksburg, the *Arkansas* had made good progress downriver, running smoothly with the current. But just as she passed the mouth of the Red River her engines began to bang and vibrate. Eight miles above Baton Rouge both failed.

All night mechanics worked to repair the stricken engines. Daylight came and Lieutenant Stevens heard the distant rattle of musketry as Breckinridge began his assault on the Federal Army in Baton Rouge. Only three Federal boats lay off the bank before the city, one of which was the *Essex*, the same boat that fired the shot that killed Albert. At that moment her guns were bombarding the Confederate infantry advancing through the streets of Baton Rouge.

Stevens ordered the crew to cast off lines. But the *Arkansas* managed to steam only a few hundred yards downriver before the starboard engine stalled. Another day had to be spent in repairs. By then the *Essex* had taken notice. Next day at first light the Federal ironclad started upriver toward the *Arkansas*. Stevens ordered the beat to quarters and the crews readied their guns.

Once again the mechanics got the engines going. The bow guns on the *Essex* had just begun to range on the *Arkansas* when her port engine went dead. Nothing the mechanics could do made any difference. The *Arkansas* turned a half-circle and the *Essex* came up firing from behind. Read answered with his stern rifles and kept the enemy at bay, but Stevens now had no choice. He ordered most of the crew ashore. A working party stayed aboard to bring up primers and shells from the magazine, which they scattered across the gun deck among cotton mattresses from the wardroom. All the guns were loaded and run out their ports.

Stevens set light to the heaped mattresses and leapt ashore as the hawsers were cut. Unmanned, the *Arkansas* drifted out into the current with black smoke pouring from her hatches and ports. Flames licked out the upper grates and spread across the gun deck, igniting the loose ammunition and loaded cannons. Shells whistled out over the river, causing the *Essex* to back away. A few minutes later the powder magazine ignited with a massive orange explosion, showering the river in burning timbers and smoking debris. What was left of the *Arkansas* sank beneath the surface of the Mississippi.

There was no news regarding the fate of the crew, whether any had been captured or killed. Days passed and I feared for Jordi and Collins and the other men. Other patients at the hospital commiserated with me, called the loss of the *Arkansas* a "disaster for the South." I would nod with great seriousness and agree. But I didn't really care what it meant for the South— the dashed expectations, the failed hope. Only when I imagined all that blood and sweat soaked into her timbers did I feel any sadness. To think of all those men bound together in the possibility of a single fate. Only then did I shed a tear at the thought of that burning wreck.

~

Doctor Hilliard set the date of my hospital release as the twenty-first of August. So I sent a note to Martha to ask Cope if he'd bring the wagon to come fetch me. Martha had written almost every day asking if she might come visit. But I didn't want her to leave Grandfather and have to make the long journey. I felt the shock would be some easier to take at home—for all of us.

I had fewer letters from Liz.

"We just write the same things," she moaned in one of her notes. "Not much happens here, after all."

In each letter Liz would ask for news of Jordi. I wrote to her about the *Arkansas* and how there'd been little word of the crew. "Maybe he's just having a high old time dancing the Virginia reel at one those big Louisiana plantations," she wrote, but I could sense her anxiety.

I let Lydia read a few of my sisters' letters.

"Just local gossip," I warned her. But Lydia seemed to enjoy them, especially those from Liz.

"I feel like I know her already," she said.

~

Before the *Arkansas* had set sail the ship's clerk had sent me a note to say that my last pay packet and discharge papers waited in a War Department office in the courthouse. I had only to sign for them. Doctor Hilliard offered to drive me up to the courthouse in his buggy and then take Lydia and me for lunch in town. I dressed in my Sunday suit. Eli helped me clip up the empty trouser cuff.

They picked me up at the front entrance. It was my first trip off the grounds since arriving. Seeing the passing houses and the busy streets was a relief after the same four walls of the hospital. All seemed back to normal now with the Federals gone.

Doctor Hilliard let me off at the front entrance of the courthouse and pulled the buggy under a shade tree to wait. I hobbled up the steps to the big new building with its massive Greek columns and tall clock tower. Inside the foyer I asked a porter for directions to the office. People stared openly as the tips of my crutches squeaked across the marble floor. I climbed another flight of stairs and reached the top, drenched in sweat. The local office of the Confederate War Department lay down a short corridor. The door was open, and two clerks in gray uniforms stood talking before an open window with a view out across the river. One of them—a short, fat officer with long, thin sideburns and a fussy red sash at his belt—took note of me in the doorway. I waited quietly in the hall but they just kept talking and laughing.

Eventually the short one turned to me in irritation. "Do you need something?"

"My discharge papers."

Only then did he seem to notice my leg. "Right," he grunted. "Name and command."

"Sam Wood from the *Arkansas*."

The taller officer looked up at me with sudden interest, but the fat one remained unimpressed. "Sorry. That's Navy Department. Nothing to with this office."

"But I was told—"

"Don't matter what you were told."

"Hold on," said the tall officer. "Something did come."

He dug among a messy pile of papers on his desk and pulled out an envelope. "Here."

The fat officer slit it open with a silver letter knife and pulled out some papers.

"Just what am I supposed to do with these?" he said sourly to no one in particular. He then pushed the papers in front of me. "Sign here. I'll just have to send it off to Richmond and let them worry about it."

He then handed me my copy.

"I'm also due a pay packet," I said.

With that he snorted, "Do I look like a paymaster?"

"But it was supposed to be sent up with the papers."

The tall officer turned back to his desk. "I'll have another look."

"Don't bother," said the other man. "We don't handle money here."

"But if you just look," I said.

He leaned back in his chair. "Something wrong with your hearing? We don't hand out pay here. Guess you think you deserve some sort of special treatment. Well, I see a dozen boys like you every day. So you take it up with the Navy Department in Richmond."

He then turned and resumed his conversation with the tall officer. Something about overcooked eggs at Mrs. Warren's. Normally I might have argued, but I felt too worn down to care. So I left the office with only my discharge papers.

Back down at the buggy Doctor Hilliard asked, "All sorted?"

"Yes. Apart from my pay."

"You didn't get paid?"

I climbed up to the seat. "The officer told me to take it up with the Navy Department."

Doctor Hilliard turned suddenly red. He climbed down from the buggy. "Just wait here," he said, striding off toward the entrance.

Lydia shook her head. "His dander's up now. Somebody's in for it."

Five minutes later he appeared with an envelope bearing my name and containing twenty-eight Confederate dollars. Doctor Hilliard climbed into the buggy and gave the reins an angry shake. "Pig-headed son of a bitch."

~

He took Lydia and me to lunch at the Warrington Hotel, one of the finest in Vicksburg. Waiters brought turtle soup and dinner rolls warm from the oven, rare roast beef with sautéed potatoes and fresh asparagus, and blackberry cobbler with vanilla ice cream to finish. I'll never forget that meal. The doctor seemed to have a fine time, too, drinking almost a full bottle of claret and testing my Latin with rude comments about the other diners. That is, until Lydia chided him for being a bore. Just as we finished our main course, a girl with blonde ringlets and wearing a green velvet dress came into the dining room with her mother. She swept past our table with a cold smile.

"Hello, Lydia," she said, nodding stiffly. "Doctor Hilliard."

Lydia responded with the faintest flicker of acknowledgment as Doctor Hilliard rose with a bow.

"What a lovely girl Margaret Green's grown into," he said when the girl and her mother were out of earshot.

"Oh yes," said Lydia sourly. "Lovely."

Standing up from our table to go, I found all eyes on me again. I didn't know how I would ever get accustomed to the stares. Margaret Green seemed to take a special interest, her eyes narrow as a cat's. Outside the hotel I asked Lydia about her.

"A former schoolmate," she replied. "Just one of my many admirers."

~

As time drew nearer for my going away, I grew more anxious each day at the thought of leaving the hospital and Lydia, of facing my future. I began to find it hard to sleep. Nighttime on the ward only made things worse, with the constant snoring and fevered moaning all around me. I also began to suffer from a burning itch in my missing leg. Doctor Hilliard called it "phantom sensation" and said it was common, though more often experienced as pain. Nothing offered relief and some nights it drove me to distraction.

The afternoon before Cope was due to arrive, I sat with Lydia on a bench out on the grounds. She was mending nightshirts for the hospital. I tried to read Dickens but found it impossible to concentrate on the words. The lack of sleep had made me tired and irritable—or maybe that was just an excuse.

I closed the book and sighed. "I wish sometimes that shell had just finished me off."

"Stop it," Lydia said, without even looking up from her sewing. She had heard such talk before.

"Why should I?" I said.

"Do you think your sisters feel that way?" she

asked. "Do you think I do? Or that I wouldn't want Gibb back under the same circumstances?"

I wasn't sure what I wanted her to say. I looked away and muttered, "I suppose when I go you'll spend more time with the other men on the ward."

"Maybe."

"Or your friends down in town."

"What friends?" she replied.

"You must have some friends. I'm sure the boys would line up."

"Hardly. I talk too much."

I felt a sudden anger at the thought of Lydia talking to any other boy. "Maybe it's more what you say."

She looked up sharply. "Meaning what?"

"Maybe you should just keep some views to yourself."

She put down her sewing. "Like…?"

"You know what I'm talking about."

"Why shouldn't I say what I think?"

"Well, our nation *is* at war."

"Not my nation," she said. "And the war is wrong and should be stopped."

"So what are all these men dying for if it's so wrong? What did I lose my leg for?"

I wasn't sure what I believed anymore in regard to the war. I just wanted to provoke her, to make her feel sorry for me. It was childish.

But Lydia just looked straight back into my eyes. "Nothing can justify what happened to you. But the worst possible reason I can imagine would be to protect slavery, which every honest person, North and South, knows is wicked and should be abolished."

"The war's not about slavery."

"How many times have I heard that one?" she said. "You know something? I agree with you. It's not about slavery or states' rights or economics. Those are just the excuses."

"So what is it about, then?" I snorted.

"Stubborn pride," Lydia answered, without hesitation. "Though some like to call it honor. That and boredom, which is even worse. Nothing stirs the soul like a good war."

"Well, that's simple enough," I said.

"Most things are."

She looked back down to her sewing, her cheeks burning bright red. I knew I'd touched a raw nerve, but I just couldn't stop myself. "So what about your brother? Did he die for no good reason?"

Lydia's face went rigid. She stood up and without a look in my direction walked across the grass to the surgeon's quarters. I sat there boiling with anger. I threw one my crutches halfway across the lawn. Surely she'd come back out, make things up. But the afternoon slowly faded. I finally stood and struggled across the lawn on the one crutch, full of self-pity. I picked up the other and hobbled back to the ward, certain that I'd ruined things forever between us. And for what reason?

~

Martha had written that Cope would be staying the night with the Haynes Bluff cousins, not far from Vicksburg, and would start at daybreak, so I expected him about nine in the morning. I slept barely a wink that night, waking in fits of remorse. Next morning I took my packed bag out to the front portico and sat drinking coffee with Eli, watching for Cope at the gate. I told him what I'd said to Lydia the afternoon before. He frowned and shook his head.

"Do you think she'll even say good-bye?" I asked.

"Of course she will," he replied, but without much conviction.

I looked at my watch. "Cope'll be here soon. Maybe she's not even awake."

Just then Doctor Hilliard emerged from the surgeon's quarters and walked across the lawn toward the main building. He stopped to ask if I was all set, and I thanked him for everything.

"Well, do come visit us," he said and went inside to start his morning rounds. A few minutes later Lydia came out onto her porch. Instead of her usual black she wore a sky-blue calico dress trimmed in gray. Her chestnut hair was brushed down across one shoulder.

"Can I see you for a minute?" she called.

I hobbled across the grass and up the steps. She held the front door open and then pushed it shut behind me. Leaning back on the wall, she pulled me close and kissed me. I could taste the salt of her tears.

"I don't want you to go," she whispered.

"Me neither," I said. "I'm so sorry..."

But she lay a finger on my lips and whispered, "Forget about it. That was yesterday."

I pulled her close, took in the smell of her hair, her skin, felt the rise and fall of her breath. Only moments, but already memory as we drew apart and kissed again.

~

Cope arrived with Sloeberry just before nine. The horse whinnied as I approached the wagon. Cope stepped down and grasped my hand. "Good to see you, Sam."

Eli helped him lift the sea chest into the wagon bed. I turned to Lydia. Her eyes brimmed with tears. "Guess it'll have to be letters for a while," she said.

"Not for long," I said and kissed her cheek.

Cope helped me up into the seat. Lydia and Eli then walked alongside the wagon to the entrance and waved us out onto the road heading north.

August was at its very hottest as we headed down off the bluffs and along the county road. Cope asked about my time on the *Arkansas*, and I told him most of the story, leaving out what had happened between me and Albert. I felt too ashamed.

"Sounds you've had a right hard time of it," he said when I finished. "It'll do the reverend a world of good to see you in fine spirits. He's been mighty worried. And then all this raiding."

"What raiding?"

"Didn't Miss Martha write about that? he asked.

"No. Nothing."

Cope shook his head. "She must not have wanted to worry you. Best learn it now, though. We've had some Confederate soldiers coming around regular in the last month, taking chickens and pigs. Say it's their legal right to confiscate property for material support of the Confederate Army. They even went for Sloeberry one afternoon until Miss Martha came outside with the old gaming musket. She thinks folks in town are putting them up to it."

"That's just thieving," I said indignantly.

"I know. But what you gonna do? Soldiers got the guns."

"I got a gun, too," I replied. But I knew that was just talk. How could I hope to resist the Confederate government?

Cope had laid a mattress in the wagon bed with an awning to keep off the sun. Late that afternoon I lay down on it and slept soundly for three hours, better than I had for days. I awoke at sunset, just as we passed Liverpool Landing and the hotel where Read and I had rested that day we waited for the *Arkansas* to steam down from Yazoo City. It had been less than a month and a half ago, but seemed a lifetime now.

Near Judkin's Farm we took to the ridge road and just around eleven that evening arrived at Sandhill. When Cope turned the wagon up the drive, Sloeberry broke into a trot, eager for her oats.

Candles burned in the front windows of the house.

14

At dawn I awoke in my own bedroom. No one in the house was up yet. Low sunlight filtered through the trees, casting leaf patterns onto the wall opposite. Over on the desk sat my Latin texts, just as I had left them the night before my departure. My storybooks lay on the mantle, along with a brass telescope, an old raccoon skull, a pig whittled from soft pine, a jar of marbles. Atop my wardrobe, old toys, untouched for years: a tin drum and horn, a wooden sword, a castle made of cardboard with painted lead soldiers standing guard. Across the room, my washstand, pitcher and basin, brush and comb. I lay there in bed, taking in these things as if seeing them for the very first time. All of them mine, yet unfamiliar, as if they belonged to someone else.

Last night I'd had the same feeling. It was as if the tears and embraces were meant for a different Sam, and I some changeling come in his place. Grandfather looked more frail than I remembered. He had to sit again when he saw me on the crutches. I stood in front of his chair staring down at the top of his head, the parting in his white hair, as he hugged my waist. No one looked at my stump as we talked later over coffee and cake—not about war nor dead friends nor nightmares, just town gossip. No one looked at the empty trouser leg, and by not looking made it the very focus of the room. Thankfully it was late and soon time for bed.

Today will be better, I told myself, and tomorrow better still.

Bessie made me a full breakfast—bacon, eggs, buttermilk biscuits. Nothing had been stinted, even with the shortages: Half the laying hens had been stolen; only two hogs were left, hidden in pens out in the woods along with the milking cows.

"Eat up now," she said. "You nothing but a bag of bones."

Liz sat at the table with her cup of tea and dry toast. "So tell me about Lydia. Can I write her?"

"She'd like that," I replied.

"Give me her address. I'll write this morning."

Liz looked about for Martha and then lowered her voice. "Did you ever hear from Nancy Thurman?"

"Not a word," I said.

"Martha wanted to break it to you. Nancy got engaged to Frasier Melton. His daddy got him a commission at the War Department. They're going to be married in October and move to Richmond."

Liz looked for some reaction, but I just kept eating my breakfast.

"So you're not sad?" she asked.

"Not at all," I said truthfully.

"Good," she whispered. "I hate Nancy Thurman."

~

Later that morning I went with Grandfather to see the orchard. He wore his battered straw hat and walked with a cane, as his rheumatism had been giving him trouble. Most of the peaches had been picked, but I found a ripe one still on the branch. It smelled as sweet as it tasted.

"We had everyone out picking this summer, even Liz," he said. "Just couldn't find the extra hands."

Grandfather didn't say why. I didn't need to ask. Too many men away soldiering, and the rest unwilling to work in a traitor's orchard.

"Got cratefuls ready for eating out in the cool house. Do you think that hospital in Vicksburg might want some?"

"I'm sure that Doctor Hilliard would be grateful," I said.

"Good. I'll ask Cope to put some on the Vicksburg coach."

I kept waiting for him to get around to the subject of Albert and my leg. How he'd tried to stop me from going. But he never mentioned it, except to ask if I found the going hard with my crutches.

That afternoon I sat with Martha on the porch, and we shucked corn for dinner. She told me that Henry had been deployed to Atlanta to help build defenses around the city. He still wrote religiously, four-page letters twice a week.

I asked Martha about the raids.

"All the farms have been hit, but no one else we know of has had as much taken as Sandhill," she said. "Most of the raiders looked drunk. I figure they came straight from Clooney's Tavern, with locals egging them on. I'm just worried some night they'll do worse."

"Not with me here," I said.

But I wasn't sure my being home would make any difference.

~

One afternoon I heard the rattle of a buggy coming up the drive. I hobbled to the front window and looked out. It was Mr. Fitzhugh and Mr. Anders from the Academy. What an odd pair they made, walking up to the steps: Anders loping on his long skinny legs, Fitzhugh struggling to keep pace, smoothing his thin dark hair back in place over his balding pate.

I went out to greet them on the front porch.

"Sam, Sam," gushed Fitzhugh. "How are you?"

"Fine. Thank you, sir."

Mr. Anders only nodded in greeting. Fitzhugh took my hand and shook it firmly with his two. It seemed whatever contempt he might have felt for me in the past had now vanished.

"I hope we're not intruding."

THE PASSAGE

I asked them into the parlor. Martha and Grandfather joined us for a glass of cool sugared tea. Fitzhugh talked without stop, telling me how many of my classmates had now gone off to war, even Wade Walton. He spoke of how proud it made him to think of "his boys" serving the cause, bringing honor to the Academy.

"But no one will forget that you were the first to step forward, Sam," he said. "You led the way."

"And Albert," I added.

"Yes, of course. We were all terribly sorry to hear about Albert. Mr. Anders especially."

Anders said nothing, only stared down at his shoes.

Fitzhugh slurped his tea and went on. "But think how privileged you boys are to count yourselves amongst the bravest crew ever to sail. Certainly the *Arkansas* and her passage through the Union fleet will be spoken of in the same terms as Nelson's victory at Trafalgar, or the defeat of the Persian fleet by Themistocles and the Greeks at Salamis."

I could see Grandfather out the corner of my eye growing restless in his chair. I prayed he'd stay silent.

"Your bravery, your sacrifice, has brought great honor to this town, not to mention your family."

With that Martha stood up suddenly from her chair. "Please excuse me," she muttered and left the room.

"Thank you, Mr. Fitzhugh," Grandfather responded in a calm voice. "We're just glad to have Sam home again."

Anders then loudly cleared his throat.

"Yes. Of course," said Fitzhugh, looking over at Anders. "There is another reason for our visit today. You may have heard that Mr. Culver who looks after the junior school has left us to go enlist in Jackson, a hard loss to the Academy. We could advertise for a replacement, but it's unlikely to prove fruitful with so many men off to war. Mr. Anders and I wondered if perhaps Sam might like to come help out this fall. We both feel you're well-rounded academically, mature for your age, and sure to be respected by the younger boys. So what do you say to that, Sam?"

I found myself lost for words. Me, a teacher?

Anders spoke up for what seemed the first time. "No need to give us your answer today. You think it over."

"By all means," said Fitzhugh. "Send me a note."

Grandfather and I saw the two men back to the buggy. Martha came out on the porch as they headed off down the drive.

"Insufferable little man," she said.

"Now, Martha," Grandfather warned. "Mr. Fitzhugh has just offered Sam a job at the junior school."

"Could you work for him?" she asked me.

"I don't know." Grandfather put a hand on my shoulder. "Word is that Mr. Anders runs things mostly. He certainly has a greater interest in teaching. He's a good man, too. You think about it, Sam. Could be an excellent opportunity."

So that day and the next I considered their offer. I knew the weeks would soon grow long and aimless without some kind of employment—but teaching? I had always thought I might someday read law; that hardly seemed likely now with the war on.

The extra money certainly wouldn't go amiss at Sandhill. I figured teaching was worth a try. I sent a note to Fitzhugh accepting his offer. I wrote Lydia with the news, and she answered straight back saying she could easily picture me in front of a classroom.

I longed to see Lydia again. Not a minute passed when I didn't think of her, and worry about what would happen when the Federals returned to Vicksburg—as they were certain to do, probably with a large army.

Toward the end of August she wrote with the news that her father had organized a trip for them to visit her aunt in Benton that November. I was overjoyed. Benton was only ten miles from Yazoo City, less than two hours in the buggy. She said they intended calling on us at Sandhill. Lydia suspected that her father wanted her to stay on in Benton until the threat to Vicksburg had passed. 'Much as I'd like to be near you,' she wrote, 'I'll never agree to that. He needs me at the hospital.' So I had to content myself with the thought of a few days together.

November seemed an age away.

~

The sea chest with Albert's possessions and the letter to his parents still sat in the cupboard under the stairs. I dreaded the thought of taking that chest down to the Ledbetters, but I knew it had to be done. Martha helped me compose a note suggesting I call that Saturday. Next day a short reply came from Mr. Ledbetter to say that they would be pleased to see me.

Saturday came round all too quickly. I felt only dread at the prospect of the visit. Cope drove me down into town and we parked at the gate. He carried the sea chest with Albert's things up to the door.

Mr. Ledbetter answered the bell. His face looked gray and drawn, his eyes hollow. He gave me a firm hug and led us into the parlor. "Look dear," he said. "Sam is here to see us."

I hardly recognized Mrs. Ledbetter in her black dress. She must have shed thirty pounds. Flesh hung limply from her jowls, making her look twenty years older. Her eyes had no spark left in them. Seeing my crutches, she began to weep. Cope put down the box and went outside to wait by the buggy. I wished I could join him.

Mr. Ledbetter served coffee and asked how I was adjusting. Still Mrs. Ledbetter did not speak. He then opened the chest and took out the letter I'd left sitting on top of the clothes.

"It's a note from our Albert," he said and started to open it.

I reached for my crutches, desperate to leave. "Maybe you want some privacy," I said.

Mr. Ledbetter laid a hand over my arm. "Please, Sam. Stay a while. It's a great comfort having you here."

Just then Mrs. Ledbetter spoke. "Did he suffer?"

I didn't know how to answer. "Well, I was pretty badly hurt myself so I didn't..."

"Just tell me he didn't suffer."

Mr. Ledbetter had opened and begun reading Albert's letter intently. Mrs. Ledbetter gazed at me with red eyes. I had no idea what to say to her.

"It was over quickly—I'm certain," I lied.

Mr. Ledbetter then folded the letter and reached over to give it to his wife. He looked at me, his eyes brimming with tears. "Albert says that having you with him was a great comfort, Sam. That it was the only thing that made the ordeal bearable. Thank you for being such a good..."

But that was all he could get out. I felt hot and dizzy, as though all the blood had rushed to my head. The room seemed suddenly airless. I stood up, held out my hand, and said I'd be back to visit another day. I just had to get out of there. Following Mr. Ledbetter out the parlor, I noticed a black muslin still hanging over the hall mirror.

Cope helped me up into the buggy. "Are you all right?" he asked.

"Fine. Let's go," I said.

Mr. Ledbetter stood in the open doorway and waved. But nothing stirred in the curtained front window as we pulled away.

~

Around that time word came that Mr. Pendleton at the mercantile had received a telegram saying his son Tom had been killed in a skirmish somewhere in East Tennessee. No one in the family, apart from Cope, had spoken to Mr. Pendleton since that day he had turned Grandfather away after the death of his older son, Justin. I think the loss of that friendship grieved Grandfather more than any of the other snubs from town.

It was a few nights later that I was awakened by the sound of shouting and gunshots. I leapt from my bed in alarm and fell to the floor. Crawling to the window, I peered out to the front yard. Over a score of men, some holding burning pine knots, whooped and hollered up at the house, the hooves of their horses tearing at the grass. A wagon rattled up the drive. Some of the riders wore hats pulled low and neckerchiefs up over their noses to hide their identities. In the light of the torches, I made out a few Confederate cavalrymen, one of whom swayed drunkenly on a tall gray horse. Just then I heard the front door splinter open. "Oh, Reverend!" someone called.

Heavy footsteps thumped across the floor and something fell over with a crash of glass. I reached for one of my crutches and a loaded shotgun I kept by the bed. I hobbled out into the upper hall just as four men rushed up the stairs. A big man in a Confederate uniform with corporal stripes rushed for me and snatched away my gun as I tried to level it.

"Give me that, boy. Before you hurt somebody."

Two other men in regular clothes with their faces hidden appeared in the hall, dragging Grandfather by the arms. He was in his nightshirt and did not put up a struggle.

"Let him go," I shouted and hobbled toward them but the soldier kicked my crutch away, and I fell against the wall. I heard Liz scream down the hall. I struggled to rise again. "Leave her be!" shouted the corporal. "That's not our business here."

A soldier appeared out of her room and followed the others with Grandfather down the stairs. Martha and Liz ran out into the hall and helped me up.

"Get me my other crutch," I said. Liz brought it to me from my room. I then went down the hall to Father's old study. Inside a locked sea chest he kept his old navy revolver. I couldn't find any ammunition but hoped maybe the threat would be enough.

Outside on the porch two soldiers now held Liz and Martha. Some of the other men had brought Cope and Bessie from their cabin. The big corporal stood up on the bed of the wagon, clutching Grandfather, who looked thin and frail in his flimsy nightshirt. I staggered out onto the porch, shaking with fury. I pointed the pistol at the highest ranked of the cavalry officers, a captain. My hand shook so much I couldn't have hit a barn even if the gun had been loaded.

"Let him be," I shouted. "Or somebody's getting shot."

But the big corporal just jumped off the wagon and ran up onto the porch without the slightest hesitation.

He pulled the gun out my hand and slapped me so hard I fell onto the floorboards. "You just won't take a minding," he said.

"Damn you, Willis!" shouted the cavalry captain. "That's no way to treat a veteran."

He then walked his horse over to the porch. "We got no quarrel with you, son. Just with traitors." The captain then turned his horse away. "Get on with it," he said.

So the corporal returned to the wagon bed and shouted out to the mob: "We may not be a legal court of law. But there's more than one law in this land."

And the men hollered agreement.

"Old man," said the corporal. "You are accused of treason against the Southern cause. How do you plead?"

The night was cool and Grandfather stood there shivering with his head bowed.

"I'll take your silence to mean guilty."

A few men laughed. The corporal pulled out a knife. Martha and Liz turned away screaming. I shouted to stop, but he only grinned and tore the knife down the back of Grandfather's nightshirt. The other soldier yanked it hard, nearly pulling Grandfather off his feet. The cloth ripped away, leaving him naked, his body little more than skin and bone. The corporal then lifted a canvas tarp off a smoking bucket of hot tar. He dipped a large brush into the tar and slapped it onto Grandfather's back, causing him to cry out in pain.

"Sorry, Reverend. Is that a mite too warm?"

The man then slowly smeared Grandfather in tar from head to toe as the mob cheered. I lay on the porch, watching with helpless rage. The corporal's assistant produced two old feather-down pillows, which the corporal ripped open with his knife and poured out over Grandfather's head.

"Now you look like the chicken shit you are," someone shouted from the crowd.

The corporal poked Grandfather again with the brush. "Turn around for all your neighbors to see."

But it wasn't my Grandfather anymore up there. Just some small, pathetic creature, black as pitch, eyes wide with fear.

"Turn, dammit!"

The creature then shuffled in a small circle as the mob hollered abuse.

"That's enough!" I screamed to the captain.

But he either didn't hear or wouldn't listen. Just then I noticed someone in the crowd looking up at me. In an instant I recognized him, even with the hat pulled down and the neckerchief over his face. Tall and shapeless, with rounded shoulders. I was accustomed to seeing him with an apron over his clothes. It was Mr. Pendleton. He saw the recognition on my face and turned away quickly.

"So what now?" shouted the corporal to the mob.

"Hang him," someone called. A few others hollered in agreement, but most went silent. There was a kind of shuffling reluctance among the men, a sense that things had already gone too far.

A rope was thrown over an oak bough and a chair brought from the house. Two soldiers stood Grandfather up on the chair and pulled the noose over his head. Liz screamed. Martha wailed loudly. "No. Please God, no."

But the captain just sat quietly on his horse and watched. Again the corporal raised his hands for attention and turned to his victim. "Mister," he said, "you got one chance left. Pledge allegiance to the Confederate cause and be quick about it."

Grandfather muttered something.

"Speak up!" shouted the corporal.

"I could do that," Grandfather repeated, his voice stronger, clearer.

"Do it then!"

He shook his head. "Even if I did, you and everyone here would know it to be a lie. So what's the point?"

"To save your miserable life."

"My life's not worth much," he said in his old church voice. "But if you think hanging an old man in his front yard will further your cause or ease your grief, go ahead."

"Damn for sure it will!" somebody yelled, but fewer in the crowd responded this time.

"Sounds like a Yes to me," said the corporal.

"Wait!" I shouted to the captain, and tried one last ploy. "Commander Isaac Newton Brown is a close personal friend of this family. I promise that unless you let my Grandfather go and leave this property now, each soldier involved—"

But the captain interrupted me. "Enough, Corporal! Let him down."

The soldier looked back, drunkenly petulant. "But sir. The will of the people—"

"Now!"

The soldiers pulled off the noose. Cope pushed out of the arms holding him, and he and Martha ran to help Grandfather down off the wagon. Like a brush fire doused with rain, the rage went out of the mob. They all quietly mounted their saddles and rode off into the night.

Bessie lit a fire and drew up buckets of water to heat in the big iron kettle. Cope put Grandfather in a tin bath and scrubbed at his skin with soap and a brush, trying to get off the worst of the tar. Grandfather sat in shocked silence.

Out in the front hall Martha knelt down, picking up shards of glass from a Venetian fruit bowl that had belonged to our mother. It had been shattered when the men first burst in.

"Tomorrow I'll go see the sheriff," I said.

But Martha just shook her head. "How do we know he wasn't one of them?"

"I saw Mr. Pendleton out there." I whispered.

"So did I," she said.

Later Cope helped me gather up every gun on the place. We brought them out to the porch along with all the shot and powder we could find. All the rest of that night I sat vigil in a rocker with a shotgun across my knee.

The sky was black and starry, the air unmoving but

alive with the hum of crickets and katydids. Sitting there alone I turned everything over again in my mind, all that had happened over the last year, over the last few hours. Was this the great nation we fought to save? A nation where to speak—even to think—"wrongly" brings a mob? Some in town would condemn what happened to Grandfather as pure lawlessness.

But were armies anything more than mobs? Were wars anything other than a failure of law, of reason? Had I fought to save something—or was the object just to be in the fight? Did it all count for nothing? So did my mind wander over those quiet hours. None of the riders returned, and I awoke later with dawn breaking across the cornfield.

After breakfast I went up to see Grandfather. He lay on his bed shivering with a fever. Raw red patches covered the exposed skin on his face and arms where Cope had scrubbed away the tar. They reminded me of the injured men from the *Arkansas*, burnt with gunpowder.

"How are you doing?" I asked.

"Been better," he said with a shudder. "I suppose this was bound to happen sometime. You were right."

"I haven't been right about anything," I muttered.

He seemed not to hear me. "They could have burned down the house. Murdered us all. Maybe I deserve to hang. Maybe I am a traitor, a coward."

"No!" I cried, not intending the anger in my voice. "Don't ever say that! There's no braver man I know."

He looked up at me in surprise. A tired smile spread across his face. "Thank you, Sam."

I leaned over and kissed his forehead and left him to sleep.

All day and most of the next night I kept my vigil out on the porch, waiting for a mob that never returned. The next afternoon I saw the dust of a wagon coming up the road. I pulled back the hammer on my shotgun and waited as it pulled to the front of the house. It was Mr. Pendleton.

I shouted for him to keep his distance, but he climbed down with his hands raised.

"Just brought your regular order," he called out, "and some letters from the post office. Most of them from Vicksburg. Thought I'd save you the trip into town."

He walked up onto the porch and held out the bundle of letters.

I lowered my gun.

He put the letters on the top step. Looking up into my eyes, he suddenly broke down in tears. "Sam," he choked. "Can I speak to the reverend?"

Grandfather came out onto the porch and gently took Mr. Pendleton's elbow. He led the sobbing man into the house and down the hall to his study. In among the bundle I found three letters from Lydia and one from Doctor Hilliard, thanking us for the peaches.

～

Three and a half months after leaving Yazoo Academy as a student, I returned as a master. That morning Mr. Anders introduced me to my charges: twenty-seven boys, aged from six to eight. My first lesson was math, sums for the younger boys and long division for the older. Mr. Anders taught senior physics two doors down and instructed me in front of the class to send a pupil for him at the first hint of misbehavior. But I had little trouble with the boys apart from the curious stares.

Just before recess that morning one of the bolder eight-year-olds, Daniel Tyler, raised his hand.

"Sir, begging your pardon. But did it hurt?" His eyes were on my empty trouser leg. A gasp rose from the class.

"Well, it didn't exactly tickle," I replied.

Tyler turned bright red, and a few of the other boys giggled.

"But it does itch sometimes," I added.

And I explained to them the mysteries of phantom sensation. The class listened so intently that they missed the bell. But this incident seemed to break the ice. Over the next days and weeks my nervousness vanished, and I grew to enjoy the early morning rise and first period with "my boys." My only dread was that this war might last long enough to suck them in as it had so many other Yazoo boys.

~

Soon the hot damp weather of late summer broke and cool air blew down from the north. I welcomed the change in season as it meant I'd soon be seeing Lydia again. One chilly Sunday afternoon in late October I sat at my desk at home, marking lesson books. Martha's fiancé Henry had come home on leave from Atlanta, and he was down in the parlor with Martha, Liz, and Grandfather. Out the window of my bedroom I could see over the fields and woods, brilliant with the reds and golds of leaves on the change: dogwood, sycamore, maple, oak. I spotted a farm wagon toiling up the Benton road from town. It stopped at the end of our drive, and a man jumped down from the seat next to the driver, who carried on up the road. He looked thin as a scarecrow, dressed in ragged gray with a slouch hat. He shouldered a haversack and headed up the drive.

I left my work and went down the stairs, picking up the loaded shotgun by the front door. The stranger had taken a shortcut across the corn stubble. I stood on the porch with the shotgun over my arm. The man's hat was pulled low over his eyes, hiding his face as he walked across the yard toward the house.

"Stop right there, mister!" I shouted.

The stranger looked up and pulled off his hat. It was Jordi.

"Some damn welcome, " he said.

He climbed up onto the porch and slapped away my outstretched hand to give me a rough hug. "Told you I'd come."

I pushed out of his arms for a look. He was lean and tan, and seemed to have grown a couple of inches. Never had a face been a more welcome sight. I put a finger to my lips and motioned him to follow me inside. We crept into the hallway and I opened the parlor door a crack. Inside, Martha sat on the sofa, unraveling one of my wool jerseys, winding the yarn around Henry's outstretched arms. The fire was banked and on either side sat Liz and Grandfather, both reading. I pushed open the door.

"Look who's just wandered off the road."

Jordi stepped into the opening. Liz looked up, first in shocked surprise and then with a broad grin, her face a picture. Grandfather began to chuckle. Martha pushed the jersey and darning needle into a perplexed Henry's lap. She rose and held out her hand to Jordi.

"Please. Come into the warmth."

Author's Note

S am Wood, his family, and many of the characters in this book are fictional, but the story of the CSS *Arkansas* is a true one. The battles and events depicted here involving the Confederate ironclad are based on real accounts by crew members and other diarists and writers of the time. Some particular details have been altered or invented for reasons of plot, but I have attempted to be as true to the period as my sources allowed.

Final preparations on the CSS Arkansas, 1862.

The rebel ram Arkansas *running through the Union Fleet off Vicksburg, 1862.*

BIBLIOGRAPHY

Below is a list of several primary and secondary sources, all of which make fascinating reading.

Brown, I. N. "The Confederate Gunboat *Arkansas*." *Battles and Leaders of the Civil War,* vol. 3. New York: The Century Company, 1884–1888.

Campbell, R. T. *Southern Thunder: Exploits of the Confederate States Navy.* Shippensburg, PA: Burd Street Press, 1996.

Foote, S. *The Civil War: A Narrative—Fort Sumter to Perryville.* New York: Vintage Books, 1986.

Gift, G. W. "The Story of the *Arkansas*." *Southern Historical Society Papers* XII, nos. 1–2 (1884).

McPherson, J. M. *Battle Cry of Freedom*. New York: Oxford University Press, 1988.

Morgan, S. *The Civil War Diary of a Southern Woman*. Edited by Charles East. New York: Touchstone, 1992.

Konstam, A. *Confederate Ironclad 1861–65*. Oxford UK: Osprey Publishing, 2001.

Read, C. W. "Reminiscence of the Confederate States Navy." *Southern Historical Society Papers* I, no. 5 (1876).

Still, W. N. (ed). *The Confederate Navy: The Ships, Men and Organization, 1861–65*. London: Conway Maritime, 1997.

Wyatt-Brown, B. *Southern Honor: Ethics and Behavior in the Old South*. New York: Oxford University Press, 1982.